⟨13⟩

THE GIRLS OF CANBY HALL®

HERE COME THE BOYS

EMILY CHASE

SCHOLASTIC INC.

New York Toronto London Auckland Sydney

ISBN 0-590-33685-1

12 11 10 9 8 7 6 5 4   5 6 7 8 9/8 0/9

Printed in the U.S.A.   06

THE GIRLS
OF CANBY HALL®

HERE COME
THE BOYS

THE GIRLS
OF CANBY HALL®

CHAPTER ONE

It was snowing huge, gloppy drops of cold, wet sleet at the Boston airport when Faith Thompson, Dana Morrison, and Shelley Hyde — roommates and best friends — got off the plane from Florida, where they had spent the term break.

It was snowing even harder as they rode in the back of a school van — through Boston, then out into the Massachusetts countryside to Greenleaf. Through the tiny town, down the road to the campus of Canby Hall, the girls' boarding school where they were all juniors.

By the time the van passed through the big wrought iron gates to the school, they could barely see outside past the sheets of rain that were covering the windows.

"Sure is nice to be back up north," Dana said sarcastically. "If sun gives a person a tan, maybe snow takes it away. If so, mine'll be all gone before I have a chance to show it off to anybody."

"Not mine," joked Faith, who was black. "Of course, I had a head start on you two."

"All I got was a burn that's already peeling off," moaned Shelley, who was blonde and fair and constantly worried about some aspect of her appearance. Usually she was worried that she was too fat. She wasn't really, just more rounded than her two tall, lean roommates.

"Oh, Shel," Dana said supportively. "You look cute. The sun brought out all your freckles."

"Argh," Shelley said. "Freckles. One of my big assets."

But by then Dana had slipped away from the conversation. The whole ride back she had been drifting in and out of her own thoughts. Some were snuggly thoughts. Like about Randy. He wasn't the boy of her dreams, but he was such a rock of stability in her life. Always there through thick and thin. She would get to see him tomorrow and, after two weeks away from him, she was looking forward to it.

Other thoughts tumbling around in her head were more disturbing. Her father and his new wife, Eve, were about to have a baby. Although the idea of a new little stepbrother or sister kind of tickled her, she worried that a new baby would take a lot of her dad's attention away from her. Dana already missed him so much since he had moved out and split up with Dana's mother. Now he was likely to be totally distracted.

"Hey! Earth to Dana!" It was Faith, pulling at the sleeve of Dana's jacket, urging her out of the back of the van, which had pulled up in front of their dorm, Baker House.

"Okay, okay," Dana said, jumping out with a shiver. The jacket she was wearing, which had seemed way too heavy in Fort Lauderdale, now seemed way too little protection against the raw, wet New England evening they had come back to. "I wonder if we're too late for dinner?" Dana said, pulling her suitcase out after herself.

"Oh, I hope not," Shelley said. "I'm starving. I dieted and exercised so much to get into that new bathing suit that two weeks later I'm still hungry." She paused, then said wistfully, "Maybe they got a new cook over the break."

"We couldn't be that lucky," Faith said. "If anything, the food will be worse than ever. I hear they use these vacations to drag old stuff out of the freezers and stockrooms. Stuff they don't want anyone to see. By the time we're back here, they've got the mystery stuff submerged in G.G. — generic gravy."

"Boy, is this bag heavy," Dana groaned. "I don't remember it being this hard to lug on the way down. Maybe I'm just more tired tonight."

"No," Shelley said. "It's probably the coconuts."

"What coconuts?" Dana asked.

"The five coconuts I didn't have room for in my carry-on and was sure you wouldn't mind if I put in your suitcase."

Dana set the bag down and was just about to lunge at Shelley to give her a fake throat throttle when she stopped midmove. What stopped her was seeing a huge pile of luggage and stereo equipment and sports gear, along with an old easy chair and some lamps. This stuff was taking up nearly half of the small lobby.

"Somebody's moving in," she said, puzzled. "That's odd. They've never admitted girls in the spring term before."

While Dana was speaking, Faith had put down her bag and walked over to the mountain of belongings. With one hand she picked up a huge black high-top basketball shoe, with the other a pair of boxing gloves.

"If these are girls," she said slowly, "we've got some very interesting chicks moving in here."

Shelley was the first one to say what they were all three thinking by now.

"Boys," she whispered breathlessly. "They're letting boys into Canby Hall!"

CHAPTER TWO

"But why would they let boys in?" Shelley asked the others.

"And how many of them are there?" Dana wondered.

"And what are they like? What kind of guys would let themselves in for being guinea pigs?" Faith mused.

"I guess we'll have to wait until it's announced. Probably at Assembly tomorrow morning," Shelley said.

"No," Faith corrected her. "We'll only have to wait until we see Casey. She was supposed to get back yesterday. By now, she for sure has complete dossiers on every one of these guys. The CIA really ought to hire that girl. She manages to find out everything about everybody around this place."

Casey Flint, a towheaded streak of energy and trouble, was the roommates' best pal. Her parents were wealthy art dealers who spent most of their time traveling, and so she hardly ever saw them. They had been in Palm Beach, though, when the girls had been down in Florida, and so she had left her friends a few days early to visit her family before heading back to school.

The roommates didn't have any trouble finding her. When they got up to 407, their room — with its black walls (an inspiration from fall term) and "floor island" beds (the frames long ago consigned to the basement) — Casey was already there. She was sitting at Faith's desk, her feet tucked under her, her nose stuck in a novel.

"Casey!" Shelley exclaimed. "What's the word!?"

She looked up at them calmly and dead-panned, "I assume you are inquiring as to whether Mr. Kreevitch got around to fixing those showerheads in the john while we were on break."

"Casey," Faith said, walking over and grabbing her by the collar of her rugby shirt, "you have exactly two seconds to deliver the info, or we are going to have to hold your head under one of those showers until you do."

"Okay, okay," Casey said. "There are three of them. The board of trustees thinks going co-ed might be a way of filling the coffers of old Canby Hall. But they didn't want to leap into things. This *is* an old New England boarding school, after all. Everything has to be done with restraint. So this term, they're letting these three in on sort of a trial basis."

"Well?" Shelley asked, "what are they like?"

"One's gorgeous," Casey said, then added, looking up at Faith, "and black."

"I don't know why you're looking at me," Faith said. "If you remember, I already *have* a boyfriend."

"I know you're crazy about Johnny," Casey said. "I'm just saying that when you see this guy, you're going to have a major ecstasy attack. I'm only telling you so you can prepare yourself and call 911 first. Have the paramedics on hand."

"What about the other two?" Faith asked, dodging.

"One's got dark, wavy hair and freckles. Kind of cute. The other guy, though, is Nerd City. Mr. Science. He wears one of those plastic pocket protectors with a bunch of pens in it. His glasses have so much lint on them that he needs a set of wipers. Every piece of clothing on his body is the wrong size. Some parts are too small, some too big. He looks like he's fighting a major battle with his hair — and losing. His name is Keith. I know because he is the only person I have ever seen at this school who actually put on one of those nametags they give you in the orientation packet."

"Where are they putting these guys?" Dana was curious.

"Here. In 407," Casey said with a straight face. Faith grabbed her by the collar again, and started tickling her for good measure, and she caved in. "All right. All right. They've cleaned out the old maid's quarters in the basement."

"What maid's quarters?" Shelley asked. "What maid?"

"I guess they used to have a dorm maid in the old old days," Casey said. "You know. To dust and arrange flowers and announce gentlemen callers."

"How did you get all this information?" Shelley asked, clearly impressed.

Casey just gave her the Knowing Eye.

"Shel. Do I ask you how you can act? Do I ask how Dana can sing? How Faith can take such great photos? We all have our talents, and information-gathering is mine."

"Then you probably know what's for dinner tonight," Faith said.

"I know what its says on the board. *Autumn Surprise.*"

"Oh, no!" all three roommates moaned together. "Not a *surprise!*"

"I know," Casey nodded. "The word 'surprise' on a Baker cafeteria menu is never a good sign. The surprise is never a pleasant one. The surprise, actually, is usually not revealed. Even after you've eaten it, the mystery still remains. And so I've taken it upon myself to ease your transition from the real world of food into the depths of Baker House. My mother took me to her gourmet deli in Palm Beach, and I brought back a huge goodie box. Give me five minutes and I'll set it all up. I've even got fancy paper plates and napkins. Don't tell any of the savages on this hall, though. This is just for the four of us."

"Oh, Case," Faith said, tousling her friend's hair, "you've saved us." Then she looked closer at the hair. "Case. Did you go and get a whole bunch of these hairs cut off?"

Casey just looked sheepish.

"You did!" Dana said, coming over to get a closer look.

"My mother," Casey said. "She took me to Larry Falcone. He's this big-deal stylist in Palm Beach. Every time she sees me, she fixes something she thinks has gone wrong with me. This time it was my hair. Do you think it's awful?"

"I think it's prettier than the old way," Shelley said. "It's like lots of little feathers all over your head. It's the kind of cut I'd get if I was going out with someone new and wanted to make a really sweet impression."

"Well, I didn't have it cut for any boy. I'm not on their wavelength. They all want to talk about sports and cars and heavy metal. Thanks, but no thanks." She got up and headed out of the room. "See you in five," she called over her shoulder as she left.

When she was gone, Dana and Shelley

started unpacking. Faith just lay back on her floor island with her hands behind her head.

"You know," she told the other two from behind closed eyes, "this is going to sound weird, but I've always been a little bit of a fortune-teller. And I'm telling you that Casey is going to change her mind about boys real soon."

CHAPTER THREE

Over the years, Canby Hall had acquired a lot of traditions. Some came out of its having been an all-girls school since its beginning in 1897. One of these girls-together traditions was Sunday morning brunch in the lounge of the dorm. At Baker House Sunday morning breakfast was traditionally a casual, come-as-you-are meal.

Some girls were already showered and hairstyled and ready for the day when they came down, but most arrived in robes or pajamas, fresh from bed, their hair wild from creative sleeping. This Sunday, the day before the start of the new term, was no exception. Except that, through an administrative glitch, no one had told the girls about their new dormmates.

This made for some interesting encounters as half-awake Baker girls opened bleary eyes to discover that the table by the coffee urn was

11

occupied by three amused and amazed members of the opposite sex.

Second runner-up in the Most Embarrassed Pageant this morning was Ellie Bolton, who arrived in the lounge still sporting her overnight remedy for dry skin, a Vaseline mask and lotion-coated hands stuffed into oven mitts.

First runner-up was Molly Jonas, who came down to breakfast wearing the sleepwear that had comforted her since childhood — red long johns with a button-back flap, and slippers shaped like ducks.

Hands-down winner in the Most Embarrassed Pageant, though, was Pamela Young, archenemy of the girls from 407. Because of Casey's advance warning, the roommates were able to dress up for breakfast and mischievously watch everyone else's mortification. Pamela provided the highlight of this event. She poured herself her usual cup of black coffee and peered around for a place to sit. Because she was wearing her mint green herbal mud pack, she could see even less well than on other mornings, and so just picked the closest empty seat. It wasn't until she had taken her first sip of coffee that she looked up to see who her tablemates were, and found herself facing the astonished stares of three boys.

The roommates nearly fell off their chairs laughing.

"She bolted so fast, she nearly broke an Olympic record," Shelley observed.

"Couldn't happen to a nicer girl," said Dana.

"I'm beginning to feel a little sorry for these guys," Faith said. "They're probably getting more information on The Secret Life of Girls than they bargained for."

"They *are* beginning to look a little stunned," Dana said.

"Maybe since we're presentable," Shelley said, "we should go over and make them welcome. Unweird them a little."

"Shelley?" Dana said, giving her the Curious Eyeball.

Shelley, who was dating two boys at once — Tom Stevenson, a local Greenleaf boy whom she'd met since she'd been at Canby Hall and Paul Clifford, her boyfriend back home in Iowa — looked at Dana in astonishment. "Hey, I've got more than enough to worry about in the boyfriend department. I'm just talking about being *friendly*. Really."

"Well, I don't have time to be friendly today," Faith said, then took a fast gulp of her coffee to show how much of a rush she was in. "I've got a tutoring session with Madame Sullivan. I have to convince her that I really worked on my French vocabulary over break. Otherwise, she's going to ship me back to Remedial Francais — the Dunce Bin. Why is it that I can get A's in everything else, and can't learn this language?"

"Forget French for five minutes," Dana said, pulling Faith out of her chair. "You're going to come over with us and do this. Everyone else is going to such great lengths to pretend these guys aren't here. I think it'll be cool to be the first ones to just go over real casually and say hi."

"Oh, all right," Faith said, "but let's get a move on. I really am late."

The three of them — Dana in the lead, Shelley right behind, Faith dragging along at the end — marched over to the table where the boys were finishing huge breakfasts. Stacks of pancakes. Plates of scrambled eggs. Mountains of toast. Barricades of little milk cartons.

"Boy," Dana said, teasing, "you guys are going to eat us out of house and home. Of course, the kitchen staff is probably ecstatic that someone finally tried the eggs."

"Yeah," said the guy with the linty glasses and the nametag stuck to his chartreuse sportshirt, "it looks like you girls live on toast and black coffee. You really ought to be starting the day with more protein. Not to mention riboflavin."

This ground the conversation to a temporary halt. For a long minute, no one could think of anything to say. Finally the black guy said, "If you ladies aren't in too much of

a hurry, maybe you'd like to have a few ribo-
flavins with us."

"Oh, thanks," Shelley said, "but we really
can't. Faith has to memorize her French
vocabu —" She stopped suddenly at the dis-
tinct pressure of Faith's elbow in her ribs.

"That's all right, Shel, I did that last night.
I think we've got fifteen minutes or so before
we all have to dash." She was already pulling
up a chair and so the other two followed.

The black guy made introductions.

"Name's Sheffield Adams. Everybody has
always called me Sheff, though. And these are
my fellow pioneers — Terry O'Shaughnessy"
— at this the dark-haired boy with freckles
nodded hi — "and Keith Milton." The boy in
the chartreuse shirt stood up and leaned across
the table to give each girl a zealous hand-
shake.

All three girls were thinking roughly the
same thought — that there could hardly be a
motlier crew, three boys who were so different
from one another. Sheffield seemed older —
older than the other two, and older than everyone around here. For one thing, he dressed in
a more sophisticated way than any of the guys
from Oakley Prep down the road or any of
the guys from Greenleaf. He was wearing
dove gray flak pants and a navy cotton shirt
with a pale blue cotton sweater tied around
his shoulders. His shoes and socks were the
same gray as his pants.

Terry looked like he came from someplace more wild and remote than here. His hair was longish and curly. He was wearing a soft old chambray workshirt and navy cords with a wide belt. The buckle was in the shape of a soaring bird.

Keith, who was still wearing his nametag, was much as Casey had described him, but he was so open and friendly that it kind of outweighed his being a nerd.

It was Faith — the one who until a minute ago had all that French to do — who made introductions for herself and her roommates, and started the conversation going with the guys.

"This must seem pretty funny to you, the Sunday morning sideshow," she said.

"Nobody told us to wear our pajamas," Sheff said. "We feel kind of left out."

"It's interesting," Keith said. "I always thought girls just woke up looking good. Based on this morning, though, I've figured" — and here he held out his pocket calculator for all to see — "that forty-nine percent of girls look pretty weird in the morning."

"Their secret's safe, though," Terry said. "We'll never recognize any of them when they're dressed up — without their bunny robes and ducky slippers and face mud. Hey, how'd you three escape all this embarrassment?"

The roommates looked at each other and broke into grins.

"We had advance warning," Shelley said. "We've got a friend who specializes in reconnaissance missions."

"We're going to need a few of those ourselves," Terry said. "Not only are we the first guys ever at Canby Hall, but we're also coming in so late in the game this year. Everyone else knows the ropes, and we're just dopes."

"Ah! A poet!" Dana teased him.

"Actually, I *am* a writer. But not a poet. I write stories."

"Really?" Dana said. "Well, I *am* a poet. Oh, that sounds sort of high falutin, doesn't it? I guess I should say that I write poems. I've been writing them since I was eleven."

"I've been writing stories since I was ten," Terry said. "I'm a lot better now that I know how to spell most of the words I need."

Dana laughed, then looked around and realized that she and Terry were talking only to each other, and that the rest of the table had moved on to other subjects.

"Why did you guys come here, if I can ask?" Faith was saying.

Keith flushed a deep red at this, and gulped so hard that his Adam's apple bobbed noticeably.

"Well," he said, "the truth is that my parents think I'm sort of a mole in a hole, that

I'm too interested in my classes and hobbies and not interested enough in, well, in other people. Girl people, for instance."

"Oh," Shelley said, teasing, "*those* kind of people."

"My folks just moved East from Tucson, Arizona," Terry said. "My dad's in insurance and got transferred to the home office in Hartford. This was one of the few good schools that had an opening so late in the year. They didn't even tell me until a couple of weeks ago that it was all-girls. I was all ready to try out for the soccer team."

"You could probably get on it," Dana chided. "We're last place in the league. We definitely need some extra talent."

Terry scratched his head thoughtfully, then said, "I think it would be kind of weird, being on a girls' team."

"Man, you'd better get used to weird," Sheff said. "Nearly everything is going to be a little weird for us around here. At least for a little while."

"Why did you come here, Sheff?" Faith asked.

"Oh, my mother and father think I'm getting too involved in music. They're both doctors and want me to get into medicine, too. They think playing the trumpet and listening to jazz records is the road to ruin. They found out about this experimental deal through this doctor friend of theirs who's on the board here, and I thought, well, why not? I always wanted to be surrounded by girls. Here's my chance."

"Isn't he cute?!" Shelley said to Faith when they got back to 407.

"Who? Keith? You bet. Of course, I'm a sucker for guys who wear their calculators."

"She means Terry," said Dana, who was on her own wavelength at that moment. "She means how cute his dark hair looked next to the pale blue of his workshirt."

"Oh, boy," Shelley said. "Do I detect Dana Morrison, victim of huge crushes, falling again?" When Dana didn't respond, just rolled her eyes upward, dreamily, Shelley went on. "No, I mean Sheff. Don't you think he's gorgeous, Faith?"

"Not particularly," she said, stretching her arms into her Michael Jackson-On-Tour sweatshirt.

"I thought you were the one who wanted to stop and sit down with him."

"That was before I heard that Romeo line of his. I mean really, don't make me gag. 'Always wanted to be surrounded by girls.' Give me a break. And a jazz trumpet player. Me fall for a musician? What do you girls think this is — 'The Billie Holliday Story'? Really. Now, if you two are ready, I think we ought to try to set a new pattern this term and look over the reading lists for our classes during the next ten weeks. French is going to be a killer. And I've got Henderson for biology this term. Casey had her last term and she shook a whole handful of dead worms in front of her face. To show her not to be scared of them. If she does that to me, I'll fall over in a dead faint. Come on, slow pokes, let's get going. Oh, I've got a million more important things to think about than that conceited goon. Mr. Sheffield Adams. What a jerk!"

She whooshed out the door ahead of the other two, who stood in the room for a long moment looking at each other. Shelley spoke first.

"She's crazy about him," she said.

"Looks like it," Dana said.

CHAPTER
FOUR

The first assembly of the term was held Monday during third period, just before lunch, in the school auditorium.

Dana, Faith, Shelley, and Casey met outside so they could sit together. As soon as they were inside, they spotted the new guys sitting in the back, looking like they were trying to disappear. By now, word was out on them, and the whole campus was buzzing. Here in the auditorium, everyone was turning around and craning their necks to get a look.

"Poor things," Shelley said. "It's like the monkey house, and they're the monkeys."

The four girls found seats together near the front, and sat down.

"I just love the smell of school at the beginning of term," Dana said, inhaling deeply. "It's the floor polish or something. And Mr. Simmons always has that fungy tweed jacket

of his cleaned so it's not covered with chalk
dust in the back. And I've got new notebooks
and felt-tip pens. It's all so fresh-starty."

"That'll be P.A.'s theme," Faith said. "The
fresh start of a new term."

"P.A." stood for Patrice Allardyce, Canby
Hall's severe headmistress, who had just
walked across the stage and was clearing her
throat and shuffling her papers at the podium.
She was dressed in a navy suit; her blonde
hair was swept up into a twist at the back, as
usual.

"Did you ever see one of her hairs out of
place?" Faith whispered to Casey.

"It's a wig," Casey whispered back. "Underneath, she's got a purple punk do." Casey and
Patrice Allardyce had a relationship a lot like
the snake and the mongoose. Natural enemies.
Ms. Allardyce liked things to be orderly, and
thought rules were the best way to maintain
that order. Casey liked things disorderly and
tried to bend the rules to see how far she
could go without actually breaking them.

"I noticed this morning," Patrice began,
"the fresh layer of snow covering the ground,
and I thought how emblematic this was of the
fresh start you'll be making this term."

Dana gave Faith a hard elbow in the ribs,
which caused Faith to burst out laughing.
Ms. Allardyce looked over with a withering
stare and stopped talking until Faith got herself under control.

When Ms. Allardyce started talking again, it was about the annual pancake festival coming up in a couple of weeks.

"She knows what everyone's waiting to hear about, and she's saving it until last," Dana said under her breath.

Finally, she got around to it.

"As you've all doubtless heard, we have three new students at Canby Hall this term. I hope you will make our first boys feel welcome, and give them the same considerations you would to any other incoming transfers. These considerations do not include, however, any fraternizing between boy students and girl students in any but the public areas of the campus. I hope I make myself clear. These three boys are here on a trial basis. If, at the end of the term, the administration feels the experiment was a success, it will consider admitting boys in larger numbers in the fall. If the trial is a failure, Canby Hall will go back to being the all-girls institution of learning that it has been since our founder, Horace Canby. . . ."

"Blah blah blah," Casey whispered to Faith. "I wish she'd finish so we could get out of here and get lunch. I don't see what all the fuss is about anyway. I'm not interested in any of those three bozos."

"No?" Faith said. "I thought you'd be interested in Keith Milton. You generally like guys who wear chartreuse shirts."

"Yeah," Casey said. "Especially with plaid pants. Now we'll have to stop talking about him. I'm getting just too excited." Then she stopped being sarcastic, looked at Faith hard and said, "Keith Milton. You've got to be kidding."

Dana got to her fifth period creative writing class early, and was surprised to find Terry O'Shaughnessy sitting all alone in a desk at the back of the room. She walked over to him. He didn't see her at first. He was too engrossed in what he was writing in the open spiral notebook on his desk.

"Hi," she said, as softly as she could, so as not to startle him.

Not softly enough, as he practically jumped out of his seat. They both started laughing at the same time.

"Who, me — nervous?" he said. "Hey, does your being here now mean you're in this class, I hope?"

"Mmmmhmmm," Dana said, nodding, thinking that his eyes were deep and blue as a lake.

"Are the writing classes here any good?" he asked.

"Oh, yes," Dana said enthusiastically. "Antonia Chase teaches here. She's been published quite a bit. And she's really a good teacher. The classes are like workshops. Everyone criticizes everyone else's stuff. But she keeps it all real gentle. You never go out of here licking your wounds."

"Good," he said. "My ego's as fragile as the next neurotic writer's. Say, I've got something I've been working on. I didn't bring it today because, well, I'm not sure it's ready. I wonder if you'd take a look at it for me and tell me what you think?"

"Sure," she said. "Just give it to me when we get back to the dorm." She stopped for a second. "Boy, does that feel weird saying 'back to the dorm' to a guy."

The classroom was beginning to fill up now. The girls coming in were either gawking at Terry as though he had two heads, or they were pretending he wasn't there.

When Antonia Chase arrived, though, Terry faded as the center of attention and deliberate nonattention.

"Ugh," Ms. Chase said, "I hate when they push these desks into rows. Everybody, move yours back into our circle." She talked with Terry a little, welcoming him to the class and asking if he'd brought any of his writing with him.

"Uh, no. I will tomorrow," he said, looking over at Dana.

It was this look that propelled Dana into a full-scale fantasy of her and Terry married and writing in different rooms of the same mountain cabin, with a waterfall rushing nearby. When they were done for the day, they would make a simple dinner of fish he'd caught that morning, then sit around and read each other their day's work. They lived in this mountain cabin in the summer. In the winter, they stayed in their penthouse apartment overlooking Central Park in New York City, Dana's home. In the fantasy, they were rich, successful writers.

By the time Dana tuned back into what was going on in class, Antonia Chase was going over the last assignments of the winter term.

"Ginny, I think you've got something here with this story about your aunts. I'd like a little more texture about the house they live in, though. Mary Beth, I'm intrigued by your 'Dear Diary' piece, but it gets a little gushy in spots, I think. Let me see here . . ." she said, rustling through the pages of the story, not seeing Mary Beth squirming in her seat.

"Oh, yes, here it is — 'Dear Diary, Today I saw Ron on the street. We stopped to talk, but I couldn't hear a word he said. All I could think of was how beautiful his lips were when they moved.' "

Ms. Chase looked up, realizing her mistake at reading something so personal aloud. Too late, though. Mary Beth's face was red bordering on purple, and she looked like she was trying to slink down into her turtle neck.

"Oh," Ms. Chase said. "Sorry, Mary Beth." Then she looked over at Terry, who just shrugged. The rest of the class was trying to control their giggling. "Hmmm. This is going to present a bit of a problem, isn't it?"

"I could write something about one of my more embarrassing sports fantasies," Terry offered. "But really, I think the class is eventually going to get used to me being here. I'm a guy, sure, but I'm also a writer like the rest of you. And I think we could broaden each other's experience." He paused, then looked at Mary Beth and said, "And if it's any help, I should tell you I've got three sisters. And I've sneaked looks at all their diaries."

When everyone started to laugh, it was Terry's turn to blush.

CHAPTER FIVE

It was amazing how much effect just three boys could have on a school of three hundred girls. They even began having an effect on persons outside the school.

On Tom Stevenson, for instance. By the time he came by Monday afternoon to kiss Shelley hello, he had already heard the news, and he was not a happy guy.

He and Shelley were standing in the parking lot of Baker House. They had planned to drive out to the falls for a romantic reunion, but Tom wanted to fight first. He kicked the tire of his motorcycle with the toe of his running shoe.

"Why'd you have to let guys in, anyway?"

"Don't look at me," Shelley said. "I don't run this place. And what does it matter, anyway? I don't see that three guys are such a big deal."

"Who cares if it's three or three thousand?

28

It's the principle of the thing. Look, all the time I've known you, we've had to go by all these Canby Hall rules. I can't come here during class hours. I can't go into your dorm, except the lounge. I can't have a Coke with you in your cafeteria. And now here come these privileged jerks, and they get to live in the dorm. . . ."

"In the basement, with a separate entrance," Shelley interjected. "It's not as if we're washing each other's hair every morning."

"Still. They eat with you. They go to classes with you. They study with you. They're around all the time. It's not fair. They've got an edge I'll never have."

Shelley reached out and gave Tom a pretend sock in the jaw.

"Dumbbell, what are you worried about? I'm not interested in any of them. And so what if they're around all the time? Maybe what'll happen is that we girls will get sick of them all the sooner."

He thought about this for a minute.

"I don't know. Maybe. But maybe not. And if this trial run is a big success, you know they're going to let more of these guys in, and then pretty soon this'll be a co-ed school and none of you will even so much as look at us townies."

Shelley sighed.

"You're way ahead of yourself, Tom. Besides, if Canby Hall does go co-ed in a big way, you could always transfer here."

"No way," he said, hopping onto the bike. "I'm a Greenleaf letterman in two sports. What are these guys going to do for teams?"

"Well, I hear they're trying to set up a mixed doubles tennis league with some of the girls. And they've agreed to be the cheerleaders for our field hockey team," Shelley said, climbing on behind him.

As they were about to snap on their helmets, Tom said, "You've got to be kidding me."

"Nope. Drive by the playing field and take a look for yourself."

Sure enough, as they cruised by the field, Tom slowed to five miles per hour and then stopped the motorcycle completely, his jaw dropped practically to his chin. While the girls' field hockey team was practicing, so was the three-boy pom-pom squad.

"Gimme a G," they were shouting as they shook their pompons, "Gimme an I. Gimme an R. Gimme an L. Gimme an S. Yay, GIRLS!" And with that, they fell all over each other laughing.

"Cute," was all Tom said as he ground the motorcycle into first and drove out through the campus gates.

Dana noticed Tom Stevenson's motorcycle peel out onto the main road. She could see the campus gates from the window of 407 Baker where she was curled up on the window seat with her quilt and pillow and clipboard, working on a new poem, waiting for inspiration to strike.

Dana loved poetry. She had been reading it for years, writing it all through high school. She worked hard at it, and had been the star of last summer's Poetry Intensive. She knew she had come a long way from her first poem, written when she was eleven. She could still remember every word, and still winced when she did. It went:

> When people tell me, grow up,
> I just want to throw up.

Today, though, she almost felt like she was back at that beginning. She was absolutely stumped. First she couldn't think of anything good enough to write about. Then she made a dozen false starts. The words seemed like huge boulders, impossible to move around right. And the thing was that she just had to come up with something special before tomorrow's class. She wanted to show Terry O'Shaughnessy that she was a good writer.

She looked down at his story, lying on the window seat by her feet. She had read it three times. It was really good.

"Dana!" someone called from down the hall, "Phone for Morrison!"

Dana uncurled herself and padded down the linoleum-floored hallway, past the half-open doors letting out the sounds of all the late-afternoon activities going on.

Sally Coburn and Alicia Henshaw were having about thirty of their friends in for Cokes and giggling. At least that's what it sounded like. It could just be five very good gigglers.

Mary Ann Olsen and Sara Smith were playing Lionel Richie records. Mary Ann and Sara were *always* playing Lionel Richie records. Whoever was married to Lionel Richie didn't hear more of him than Mary Ann and Sara did.

Phoebe Warrick was blowing her hair dry. Phoebe spent about as much time doing her hair as Mary Ann and Sara spent listening to Lionel Richie.

Louise Fiorello was studying. There really wasn't any sound coming from her room. It was just that Louise studied so hard that after a while, Dana really thought she could feel studying emanations coming from behind Louise's door. Louise had a single, so she could study better. It was the last room on the hall. Beyond it were the double doors that led to the stairwell. On the landing was the floor's pay phone. As Dana pushed through the doors, she could see that the receiver was dangling. She knew without picking it up that on the other end of that phone she would find Randy

Crowell, wondering why she had been back a whole day and not called him.

"Hello?" she said anyway.

"Hi, sweets. How can you have been back a whole day and not have called me?"

"Oh, they really socked the homework to us right off the bat this term. I can't believe it," she lied. The only assignment she had was the poem.

"You want to let me take you away from all that?" he said, his voice teasing.

"I'd love to Randy, but I really can't. I've just got to get a really good poem ready by tomorrow and I've got a logjam in my brain."

"Dana," he said, now with exasperation in his voice. "You've been working on one poem or another for as long as I've known you. I don't really think taking a couple of hours off is going to set literature back in any heavy way."

"Cool it, Randy," she said, ice in her tone. "I don't make fun of horses or apples or any of the things that are important to your outdoors soul. So don't you start trying to make me feel stupid about my poems. I won't have it," she said, and hung up.

Johnny Bates was walking by Pizza Pete's in Greenleaf and saw Randy standing inside the front door, holding the receiver of the pay phone, looking at it as if it had just bit him.

Johnny pushed open the door.

"You get attacked by a wrong number or something?" he asked Randy.

"Sometimes your own girl is the wrong number," Randy said, shrugging.

"Dana troubles?"

"Yeah," Randy said, "and I don't know where they're coming from."

"I'd ask Faith, but even if she knew something, I doubt that she'd tell me. Those girls have a secrecy pact with each other that's unbreakable. Oh, I do have one news flash, though. The girls of Canby Hall are now the girls of Canby Hall plus three guys."

"Oh," Randy said, but he was clearly distracted.

"You're not worried?" Johnny asked.

"Huh?" Randy said, tuning in again. "Oh, well, these guys have only been here one day, right? I don't think even Dana can fall in love that fast."

CHAPTER SIX

At precisely three-seventeen a.m. on Wednesday morning, alarms and sirens went off all over the Canby Hall campus.

"Huh?" Faith said.

"Wha?" Shelley shouted, sitting upright in her bed.

"Oh, no," Dana groaned. "Fire drill," she said as she rolled over onto her stomach and smashed her pillow over her head.

"Come on, everybody! Fire drill." It was their housemother, Alison Cavanaugh. She opened the door to 407 and stuck her head in. "All right, you three, let's get a move on. Downstairs and outside as soon as possible!"

"Let's don't and say we did," Faith said.

"Faith! What if this were a real fire?"

"Is it?"

"No. It's a fire drill."

"I've been on those before. I know which stairway to take and how to keep calm. In a real fire, I'd be great. So why can't I just sleep this one out?"

Alison put her hands on her hips and didn't say anything, just stood in the doorway and gave Faith a triple whammy look. The girls in 407 were crazy about Alison. She wasn't anybody's idea of a traditional housemother. In the first place, she was only in her mid-twenties. In the second, she was *very* hip and sensitive to the girls' needs and problems. She lived in an apartment on the top floor of Baker, a great airy space she called The Penthouse. If a girl was in trouble, she could always count on tea and sympathy up in The Penthouse.

But every once in a while, Alison asserted herself as housemother. All three girls looked up at her, standing there framed in the light from the hallway, arms akimbo, her hair disheveled from sleep, her glasses slipping down the bridge of her nose, looking imperious in the brightly colored African dashiki that she wore instead of a robe. They knew she meant business. And so they hopped out of bed and into robes and out into the hallway as fast as they could. Faith and Shelley did this seriously. Dana, however, couldn't resist the urge to be a little impish. And so, as she was on her way out, she turned and gave Alison a mock salute.

When the three of them got downstairs and outside, everyone was milling around sleepily

in their robes. And what robes! The girls —
especially the upperclasswomen who had been
around awhile — took a reverse chic stance
on robes. The worse the better. Nothing new
or stylish. Instead, everyone competed to come
up with the oldest, rattiest, most moth-eaten
robes possible.

Shelley, for instance, had a pink chenille
from the forties that she had found in her
grandmother's closet. Faith had found an
aqua quilted beauty in a thrift shop. Dana
wore an old maroon-striped piece of mange
that her father had worn in college. Casey had
a luridly colored rayon number that said
"Okinawa" on the back.

And so fire drills, with all these garish robes
gathered together in one place, was a laugh-
ably sorry sight. Tonight, though, with Terry
and Sheff and Keith standing out on the front
lawn watching this pageant of atrocious taste,
the girls felt a little silly.

Especially Faith. Double especially when
Sheff, looking amazingly pulled together for
the middle of the night, in purple sweatpants
and a cream-colored muscle T-shirt, came
over to say hi.

"We've got to quit meeting like this," he
joked.

"Why do you have your trumpet with
you?" Faith asked, nodding toward the black
horn case in his hand.

"When the bells went off," he said, "I

wasn't sure if it was the real thing or not. I
didn't want to leave Babe in there to melt to
death."

"Babe is the trumpet," Faith said.

"It's an old friend," Sheff said, refusing to
let her embarrass him.

"Will you play it sometime?" Faith asked.
"I'd like to hear. Really."

He nodded.

"Sometime," he said.

Boy, Faith thought, *this guy is Mr. Cool.
He must have a temperature of about forty
degrees*.

"What about playing now?" she said.
"We've got time to kill while they evaluate
the drill. They're not going to let us back in
for at least ten minutes."

He looked around.

"Uh, I don't think so," he said, scanning
the crowd. "This is the Top Forty set here.
Way too preppy for the blues. Too preppy
for me." He paused and then looked away as
he spoke, as if he wasn't quite speaking to
Faith. "Maybe sometime I'll play something,
but just for you."

Sheff's ultracool style threw Faith off-
balance. She grew tongue-tied, which was not
at all like her. She had a million questions to
ask him, but was too shy to say anything.
Something about how smooth and sure he was
made her all unsmooth and unsure.

* * *

Later that night, when they had all gone back to their rooms, and were going to sleep for the second time, Faith thought she heard something coming from outside. She leaped to the window and threw it wide open. She stuck her head out into the moon-bright night. What she heard was soft strains drifting up from below — a mournful horn playing an old blues song — "Blue Gardenia."

The next morning, after Shelley had gone off to an early play rehearsal, Dana was impatiently tapping her foot as she stood in the doorway waiting for Faith to come down to breakfast with her. Faith was examining herself in the full-length mirror on the back of the closet door.

"Are you becoming vain?" Dana asked. "I haven't seen you spend this much time in front of the mirror in the whole time we've been here."

Faith just kept staring at herself for a while, as if she hadn't heard the question. Finally, she said, "Dana — do you think I'm too preppy?"

CHAPTER SEVEN

Dear Maggie,
Happy Birthday, Knucklehead. Fourteen! I can't believe it. I guess I'll have to quit calling you my "kid" sister now.

I hope you get good presents. I told Mom you wanted a squooshy down vest. Dad and Eve called last week and I said you were a greedy girl and just wanted $$$. Otherwise I figured she'd just go out and get you something impossible again like the Dumbo umbrella. I'm pretty sure that, in her heart of hearts, Eve thinks you and I are about three and five years old. Other than that, I basically think she's okay. I've been trying to stop thinking of her as the "Other Woman." I mean Mom and Dad *were* split up for a long time before she came on the scene.

My present is this Canby Hall sweatshirt. I'm hoping it lures you up here for a weekend. Then you can meet our new *male* students! There are three of them. They've stuffed the poor guys down in the basement, like trolls. One's a writer. He's also cute and has dark, wavy hair. Terry is his name. You can probably detect the gooniness between these lines. Maybe I *am* a little goony. But I think he is, too. Why else is he showing me all the stories he writes? Why did he come over and sit at my table four separate times this week?

Further bulletins as they come in. Hi to the gerbil family. How many of the little critters are there now? You know, of course, that Mom's going to kill you when she finds out that your closet holds one of the world's largest private gerbil ranches?

XOXOXOXO
Dana

When she finished the letter, she stuck it in the big envelope with the sweatshirt and taped it shut and then on the back printed HAPPY YOU-KNOW-WHAT and then drew a birthday cake with candles in red marker. A pretty terrible drawing, she had to admit.

Then she changed into navy cords, a pale yellow shirt and a pink sweater vest, pulled on her running shoes, ran a brush through her long brown hair, and was out the door, the package tucked in her backpack. She'd mail it in town.

She was in a rush. She'd have to run part-way into town if she was going to make it to Pizza Pete's by five-thirty. She was meeting Randy for a quick Coke before they drove out to his family's huge horse farm and apple orchard (which Faith referred to as "The Ponderosa of Massachusetts") for dinner.

Neither of them had mentioned the phone fight, but they had been getting along pretty well in the days since. She was looking for-ward to dinner with the Crowells. They were sort of her "family away from home," even though they were practically on a different planet from her own family.

Randy and his brothers and parents around the big oak table made for boisterous meal-times. Back home for Dana, it was just her and Maggie and their mother in the dining alcove off the living room.

Randy's mother was home all day, and fixed rhubarb pies and corn casseroles, even baked her own bread. Dinners at Dana's house were catch-as-catch-can. They ate after the girls got home from school and their mother returned from the department store where she was a fashion buyer. They were heavily into frozen entrees and boil-in-bags and takeout from the Chinese restaurant down the street. Dana and Maggie sometimes did the cooking. This was usually good for a laugh. Maggie especially liked to toss the cookbook and improvise. It was Maggie who came up with the infamous Brown Rice and Peanut Butter Jambalaya.

Randy's mother fixed regular food — pot roasts and fried chicken and ham. Being at Randy's place was kind of like being at the Little House on the Prairie — odd, but sort of fun in a way. She loved how easily Randy's family had accepted her. She felt like a real sister to his brothers. Sometimes she worried, though, that it was Randy's big warm family, and his beautiful ranch, and the horses they rode all over his property, and the way he was always there for her, that she liked — more than she liked Randy, just the person alone.

It was just the opposite with Terry. He hardly ever talked about his family, or what it was like back in Tucson. The only person from back there who he mentioned much was Chris, whom Dana assumed must be his best friend.

When she got to the post office, Dana got the surprise of her day, maybe the surprise of her week. Sitting there on the wide stone steps in front of the old brick building, like two peas in a pod, were Casey Flint and Keith Milton. From the looks of it, they were in the middle of a serious conversation, but they were speaking too softly for Dana to hear what they were saying.

"Hi," she said, coming up to them. Casey jumped as if she'd rubbed her way across a carpet and touched a doorknob.

"Uh, oh, hi," she stammered.

"I'm mailing my sister a birthday present," Dana told them, then realized she didn't have to make an excuse just for showing up in front of the post office. She was just picking up on Casey's nervousness.

"It's closed," Keith said. "Today's Saturday. It closes at noon. But even if this were a weekday, you would've missed the boat. It's five-seventeen now, and Monday through Friday, the post office closes at five." He paused. "It's closed all day Sunday, in case you didn't know that. You'll have to bring your sister's present back Monday."

"I guess I will," Dana said. Sometimes Keith talked like a computer printout. "And if it's five-seventeen, I'm just on time to meet Randy, so I'd better get on my way."

Later that night, Dana came back to Baker. Shelley was still out, but Faith was back from her date with Johnny. Dana told her about Casey.

"With Milnerd?!" Faith said, incredulous. "Will wonders never cease?"

About two seconds later, Casey, her composure back in place, stuck her head in the door.

"Hey you two," she said. Then to Dana,

"Funny running into you at the old P.O. Keith has been helping me with my math a little. The guy's a brain machine, and I'm such a wimp with figures. He offered and I thought, why not, you know what I mean?" Then she yawned and stretched a little and said, "One thing about studying is that it gets me so tired I'm punchy. Guess I'll hit the hay."

When she was gone long enough so that they didn't think she would hear them — about two seconds to be exact — Faith looked at Dana and shrugged.

"Sounds like a reasonable explanation," she said.

"Yeah," Dana said. "Except they didn't have any books with them. Now maybe he was teaching her to do logarithms in her head, or they could have been memorizing multiplication tables. But my guess is that our girl Casey has got a strictly nonacademic interest in Keith."

Shelley burst through the door at this moment, breathless.

"Whew," she said. "I just made it for sign-in by about ten seconds. Alison was just locking the door." She stopped for a minute and noticed the look of unfinished conversation between her roommates.

"Something's up," Shelley guessed.

"Casey," Faith said.

"Boyfriend," Dana added.

"Who?" Shelley said, pinching both of them to make them tell faster.

"Well, let me put it this way," Faith said, "if they start going together, she'll probably get to wear his calculator around her neck. If they get married, she can Windex his glasses every night when he gets home."

"Not *Keith*!" Shelley squealed.

Faith clamped a hand over Shelley's mouth.

"Hush, girl. Casey just left here. We don't want her to hear us gossiping about this. It's just what she's worried about. We've got to be supportive. She's our best friend and as far as we know, this is her very first venture into boyfrienddom."

"But you've got to admit it's pretty amazing," Shelley said.

"Honey," Faith said. "Love is *always* pretty amazing."

CHAPTER EIGHT

Sunday morning everyone at Canby Hall woke up happy. It was the day of the annual Pancake Breakfast, a tradition since the school's beginnings.

It was the school's way of saying thank you to their friends, families, and the community of Greenleaf, Massachusetts. It was a day when nobody wanted to sleep in. Dana and Faith and Shelley took half their usual time to get up and dressed and out of Baker. Together, they ran across campus, into the grove.

A few girls who came from nearby towns had invited their families to the event, but the three roommates came from too far away to expect that — Dana from New York, Faith from Washington, D.C., Shelley all the way from Iowa. They just planned to enjoy the morning with each other and their boyfriends from town.

Faith was sort of including her little brother

47

Richard in the breakfast by mailing him a
pancake. She was going to get one hot off the
grill, pour butter and syrup over it, slip it into
a baggie, and then put the baggie into a
squooshy envelope and mark the envelope
FRAGILE PANCAKE, HANDLE WITH
CARE.

"It should be in real good shape by the
time it gets to him," Dana teased. "Crushed,
stone cold, probably poisonous. It's a present
he'll really treasure, Faith."

Faith didn't bother responding verbally to
this. She just waited a few seconds to put
Dana at ease, then tackled her onto the lawn.

"Hey!" Dana squealed. "These are new
khakis. I'm going to have mud all over me."

Shelley gave them both a helping hand up.

"Come on," she said to them. "Let's skip
the rest of the way to the grove!" The three of
them had decided awhile back that skipping
was a great thing of kidhood, and they didn't
want to stop doing it just because they were
sixteen.

Faith knew she wasn't completely crazy for
wanting to send Richard one of the special
pancakes. After all, they *were* the best pancakes in the entire world. First, they were
made with a secret batter recipe handed down
from the school's founder, Horace Canby.
Second, they were topped with both hot pure
maple syrup *and* melted butter. And third,
they were served with bacon cured on Claude

Blake's farm, and milk from Adele Higgins' Guernseys. The combination was a great New England country breakfast.

It was a tradition that the students and faculty and staff did all the work and also provided the after-breakfast entertainment. The three roommates had drawn clean-up duty as their chore. So, after eating their fill, they went and got their big black plastic bags and started clearing away the paper plates and plastic silverware and paper napkins. It was pretty easy work, except for getting stuck on the syrupy plates. Dana especially had trouble with this, and took a lot of teasing from Faith and Shelley, who started calling her "Flypaper."

They talked as they worked, with each other, with friends and their families, and with a table of very old Canby Hall alums from the class of 1925.

At one point, a little later, Faith nearly fell over laughing.

"What?" Shelley asked.

"Come on," Dana said. "Tell. You've got to let us in on the joke."

But Faith was laughing too hard. All she could do was point — at Patrice Allardyce, who was seriously ladling batter onto one of the open fire grills, wearing a high, French chef's hat.

"Wonder where the boyfriend contingent is?"

Shelley asked, looking around. She was eager for Tom to get there. The other two had mixed feelings about the arrival of the guys from Greenleaf. This would be the first time they would meet the boys from Canby Hall.

For Faith, the problem was that, although Johnny Bates was a terrific person, he was what Dana called an RTB — a Regular Teenage Boy. Sheffield Adams, on the other hand, was a highly *ir*-regular teenage boy. He was sophisticated, high-style, superconfident. Johnny was no fool. When he met Sheff, he was bound to see in a flash that any girl within ten miles would be attracted to him.

Worse, Faith worried he would see how she in particular was attracted to Sheff. She was a terrible poker player. Everything she felt showed up on her face.

Dana's worry was along the same lines. She wondered if Randy would see how much she and Terry O'Shaughnessy had in common. Although she and Randy were close, they shared few interests. He was a nature lover, she was a city girl. Terry was just much more her natural type. And the way they'd been clicking, she was pretty sure a total stranger could hear that click a mile off, let alone a potentially jealous boyfriend.

"Here they are!" Shelley shouted. It was Johnny and Tom, ambling into the clearing. They were tossing a football back and forth as

they walked. They both had spikes on. Johnny
was even wearing his Greenleaf High ski hat.
They were both clearly full of high spirits.

Shelley and Faith rushed over to say hi.
Dana wondered where Randy was. She didn't
have to wonder long, though, because suddenly, from off in the distance, there was the
pounding of hoofbeats. As they grew louder
and louder, more and more people stopped in
midsentence, or midbite of pancake, and
looked around, trying to figure out where the
noise was coming from.

And then Randy appeared, atop a huge,
sweating, gray horse, which he reigned to a
fast stop at the edge of the clearing. As the
horse snorted and danced around in place,
Randy — striking in jeans and a bright red
sweater — smiled across the sea of astonished
faces and grinned straight at Dana.

She thought her heart would burst with
pride. He looked so dashing and handsome —
like a hero out of an historical romance. She
couldn't help wondering if everyone else there
was finding him utterly glamorous.

"The Lone Ranger rides again," said a low,
sarcastic voice from just over her shoulder.

Dana turned. It was Terry, looking at
Randy as if he were the biggest gobbler imaginable. Dana's pride immediately deflated
into sheer embarrassment.

"Who's the cowboy?" Terry asked.

"Oh, just this guy from around here," Dana

stammered. "His folks are big landowners or something. They've got an orchard, I think. And they raise horses. He used to go to Greenleaf High, but I think he graduated last year."

"You know him very well?"

"Oh, no, not really. You know. You're around a small town for a while and you get to know almost everybody at least a little." She couldn't believe she was lying like this. At least, lying by what she wasn't saying — that Randy was, at least technically, her boyfriend. But she just couldn't bring herself to say it.

But what was she going to do when Randy parked his horse and sauntered over here? How was she going to explain why he had his arm draped over her shoulders if she barely knew him? (Randy *always* draped his arm across her shoulders when he first walked up to her. It was about Number Five on the list of things about him that drove her nuts.)

In the middle of her panic, though, Dana got saved by the bell. Well, by Patrice Allardyce's voice actually.

"Girls! Girls!" she shouted, waving her ladle through the air. Then Alison Cavanaugh, who was standing next to Ms. Allardyce, tugged on her sleeve and whispered something in her ear.

"Oh, yes," the headmistress corrected herself. "I mean girls and *boys*. Now is the moment to leave our guests and scurry through the forest to prepare yourselves for the Hurry

Spring Pageant." She waved them off with her ladle, as if it were a queen's sceptre, splattering Alison with pancake batter in the process.

At Ms. Allardyce's bidding, all the students rushed out of the clearing. As Dana passed Randy, she made a weird gesture which she hoped would seem like a wave to Randy, but to Terry as though she were only shooing away a bothersome fly.

As the students departed, Patrice Allardyce turned back to the guests and began her speech.

"The Pancake Breakfast has been part of the Canby Hall tradition for nearly a hundred years. The Hurry Spring Pageant, however — if I may be so immodest as to say so — is entirely my idea, and has been presented each of the seven years that I've been headmistress of Canby Hall.

"My idea was for a pageant in which the students would anticipate — in music, dance, and costume — the joyous season of nature's rebirth."

The costumes for the Hurry Spring Pageant came mostly out of the ancient wardrobe room of the drama department, a dank, dusty place where the moths were big as bats. It was from these dark recesses that the girls came up with things like a trunk of pastel tulip dresses from a senior play called *Windmill*

Girls and several mangy animal suits — a few
bears, several tigers, a two-person donkey suit
— which they adapted with homemade masks
so that they would look at least something like
forest animals — badgers, woodchucks, and
squirrels. They also found lots of long, green
velvet gowns from a long-ago production of
Oedipus Rex. These had not aged well.
Greener than their original color and greasy
from many wearings, they now looked like
they were made of damp moss. In addition,
there were *papier maché* sun globe and moon
crescent get-ups that a person could step into
and hold up with suspenders, and five frog
outfits with rubber raft lily pads.

The girls ransacked the place and wore
whatever they could find that seemed even
remotely springlike.

Each year, the entertainment in the pageant
was devised by the girls. Sometimes it got
pretty wild. One exceptional year, the girls
put on SPRING-steen! — a rock performance
done to Bruce Springsteen songs. But usually
no one was well-enough organized so early in
the term to put together anything more than
the most haphazard, impromptu show. Most
years, the girls never got down to working on
it until a few days before.

Which was part of the fun. They all en-
joyed the sloppiness of the show. It was fun
hamming it up in the terrible old costumes

and not worrying if someone missed a step or sang off-key.

This year, Dana sang in the chorale, which had snagged all the tulip costumes and sang a really corny version of "Tiptoe Through the Tulips" while a troupe of woodland animals — including Faith in white wings and a yellow strap-on beak impersonating a duck — wove their way between the singing flowers.

Shelley's part of the performance was a dramatic reading of a poem about the season. She wore a dress made up of all the scarves on the fourth floor of Baker. The effect was something like a butterfly.

The boys of Canby Hall were included in this year's pageant, too. Keith wore a black-and-yellow-striped T-shirt, and a set of Ping Pong ball antennae. He buzzed around at odd moments, doing a pretty good bee.

It was Sheff, though, who stole the show. When the last piece was over, and the entire cast came out of the trees en masse, he bounded out in a court page outfit and played a triumphant heraldic march, with soaring notes and wild exuberance.

The music buoyed everybody in the cast, and they all lifted him off the ground, carrying him away on their shoulders, passing him back as they disappeared into the grove, until the last of them set him gently down again, and he stood alone, playing a pure solo of "Taps."

CHAPTER NINE

After the guests had burst into wild applause for Sheff and for the whole pageant, the performers rushed back out from the grove into the clearing to mingle with their audience.

Dana, still in her tulip dress and brightly rouged cheeks, finally got over to say hi to Randy.

"Hey," he said, draping an arm across her shoulders, "what do you say we get away from this crowd and go for a ride?" He patted his horse on the neck.

"Gee, Randy," Dana said, trying to think fast. Terry had already asked if they could get together to go over their stories for Monday and she had said yes. "I'd love to but, but . . . I've got to go into town with Faith."

"Why?" he asked.

She hadn't expected any further questions

on this and so didn't have any further answers. She punted.

"Oh. She's . . . uh . . . getting her hair cut. She wants a new style, but not too new. She wants me along to give my opinion, so she comes out looking ahead of everyone else, but still like she comes from this planet."

Randy didn't laugh. He didn't laugh at a lot of what Dana thought were her best jokes. This was Number Four on the list of things about him that drove her crazy.

Now he just nodded. Clearly he was disappointed. But then they started talking and things went better. He told her his whole family was down with colds.

"And so that leaves me as designated runner. I no sooner get back from town with a fresh load of Kleenex and orange juice and cans of chicken soup than someone wants a Snickers or a magazine and I have to drive back. I'm beginning to feel like Florence Nightingale."

"You *would* look kind of cute in one of those little white caps," she teased.

Just then, Terry spotted her from across the clearing. He waved and started over.

Oh, no, Dana thought, but when he got there, he didn't act a bit surprised to find her talking with someone she had just said she hardly knew. Terry introduced himself to Randy, who was open and friendly as usual.

This was one of the really good things about him.

"I've got to get out of this woodpecker get-up," Terry said. "I feel a little ridiculous." Then he turned to Dana and said, "So then. Meet you in the lounge in half an hour?"

Before Dana could think of a really good way out of this predicament, Randy was up in the saddle and tearing out of the clearing so fast that Dana didn't see what was happening until it had already happened.

"Something I said?" Terry asked.

"No," Dana said, disgusted with herself. "Something I did."

"I don't want to get you in any trouble."

"You didn't," she told him. "I did that all by myself." And then she thought, *At least now Terry knows what's going on, that I'm throwing my romance into jeopardy for him.*

"I know," he said thoughtfully. "Sometimes when you're really working on your writing, it takes time away from your friends. They get angry."

Meanwhile, Faith was having her own set of troubles. When the pageant was over, she went back to talk with Johnny and Tom and Shelley. Pretty soon, though, the guys were tossing the ball around again and Shelley was talking with Alison, who had come over to compliment her on her reading.

So Faith took the opportunity to sneak over and tell Sheff how terrific she had thought his solo was.

He was sitting by himself on a fallen log on the other side of the clearing. He was all alone and looked very much the spectator at this event full of old friends and family.

"Penny for your thoughts," Faith said, sitting down next to him.

"This one's worth a dollar," he said, not looking at her.

"Then I'll have to owe you," she said. "I never carry that much cash with me."

"I was thinking that it's lucky you've got that nice football-playing boyfriend."

"Lucky for who?"

"For you, girl," he said. "Otherwise I'd be making a play for you, which would completely mess up your life. You'd be so crazy about me that your grades would slip and you'd just be going around all the time in a romantic fog and all your friends would be sick of you. It would be awful. Really. So I'm glad you've got that football player."

Ordinarily, Faith was pretty fast with a snappy comeback to almost any remark. But this little speech of Sheff's stopped her dead in her tracks. For a minute or so, all she could do was stare at him in amazement.

Finally, though, she pulled herself together, stood up and walked away. When she'd gotten about five feet, she came back, faced him, and said, "You are the most conceited boy I've ever met."

And then she walked away again. As she kept going across the clearing, she began to understand why his remark had outraged her so. It was true.

Suddenly, someone was grabbing her arm.

"Hey! Faith! Are you in there somewhere?"

Faith turned. It was Shelley.

"Oh, Shel. Sorry. I guess I was lost in space."

"Well, beam yourself down," Shelley said, excitement in her voice, "and try not to look like you're looking at them."

"At who?"

"Behind you," was all Shelley would say.

"Shelley. How am I going to turn completely around to look, without looking like I'm looking?"

"I know," Shelley said. "You can twirl around, like you're just happy."

Faith looked at her with a look that said, "Are you kidding?"

"Okay," Shelley said. "You're too cool to twirl. So you'll just miss the couple of the month. Really, Faith, take my word. This is worth a twirl."

"It had better be," Faith said, going into a twirl.

What she saw as she twirled was definitely worth the indignity.

There, sitting side by side on top of one of

the picnic tables were Keith in his bee suit, Ping Pong ball antennae bobbing, and Casey. She had worked up her own spring costume. She had worn long underwear, then brushed herself with library paste, then rolled around on fifteen bags of cotton balls she had poured onto the floor of her room. When anyone would come up to her and ask what her costume was — and nearly everyone did — she explained to them that she was pollen.

So it was the bee and the pollen on that picnic table, and they were — and this was the part worth twirling for — holding hands and looking deep, deep into each other's eyes.

"So?" Shelley prompted Faith. "What do you think?"

Faith turned back and shrugged. Her usual cool had returned.

"Well, clearly it's a new method of math tutoring. The tutor transfers his knowledge of algebra to the tutee by way of osmosis — through the palms."

CHAPTER TEN

W hat's this?" Shelley asked, holding up a can without a label. She had found it rummaging around in the 407 "goodie box" looking for a late-night snack.

"Oh," Faith said, looking away from the mirror for a moment, "I picked that up at the grocery store the other day. They had a whole basket of them on sale."

Shelley shook the can, then held it up to her ear.

"It's not ticking," she said. "Faith, do you have even a clue as to what's in here?"

"Not sure," Faith said distractedly. She was having trouble with her new glitter eye shadow crayon. This was the third try she'd made at getting her eyes to look like those of the model in the magazine open on the dresser in front of her.

"Maybe it's cream of mushroom soup," Shelley said wistfully. That was her favorite.

"But maybe it's minced worms," Dana said, teasing. She was studying the worm dissection diagram in her biology book.

Shelley, whose appetite usually won out over all obstacles, eyed the can a little longer, but was finally defeated by the remote but horrible possibility that it actually *was* full of worms.

"Oh, well," she said, and sighed. "I guess I'll have to burn off some allowance at the machines. I think I saw some Oreos in there yesterday. Anybody else want something?" she said as she was going through the pockets of her jacket for change.

"Can you get me a Tab?" Faith said.

"Me, too," Dana said, putting her book down at the foot of her bed and then lying back and rolling onto the floor, where she started doing leg lifts. "Studying gets my muscles all cramped up. Actually, I think studying is kind of generally unhealthy. People our age, in our formative years, should do much less of it."

After Shelley had left, Dana sat up and turned to Faith and said, "I'm dreading cutting open my worm tomorrow."

"We did it today," Faith said.

"It probably wasn't all that gross when you got down to it," Dana said, looking for moral support.

"Oh, it was much grosser," Faith said, then, "Do you think I look young for my age?" She turned toward Dana and stepped closer, as if Dana had never seen her before, and she wanted to give her a good look.

"That depends," Dana said. "How old are you? If you're forty-two, then that eye shadow makes you look a little young. Forty-one maybe."

"Thanks," Faith said, sarcastically.

"Well, really, don't you think that stuff's a little *disco* for a Tuesday night in the dorm?"

"I'm just practicing," Faith said. "I'm trying for something new. I've worn my hair in this same short Afro since the beginning of junior high. I never wear makeup. I look like a kid. I'm sixteen. I should start thinking about a new image."

"But why?" Dana said. "For what? Or should I say, for whom?"

"I don't know what you're talking about," Faith said huffily.

"Of course you do. Please. Don't be fake with me, Faith. It insults our friendship. You're crazy about Sheff."

"I hate, loathe, and despise Sheffield Adams."

"Yes," Dana said, "and you're also crazy about him."

Faith heaved a huge sigh and sat down on the bed next to Dana.

"It's so weird," she said. "I think he's a completely conceited jerk and I avoid speaking to him every time he's around. And then

I think about him night and day. I mean, is that weird, or what?"

"I don't know," Dana said, stopping her exercises and looking Faith hard in the eye. "I think it's really pretty normal. Or at least normally abnormal. You know, I have almost no understanding of how I feel most of the time. And it's always changing. Like with Randy, poor guy. One minute I like him. The next minute I wish he'd move to Australia. The next minute I think of how sweet and steady he is and I like him all over again.

"He's getting pretty sick of this," she went on. "It took me a lot of heavy-duty explaining and apologizing to get off the hook for lying to him at the Pancake Breakfast. He's still suspicious about me and Terry, which he has a right to be, I guess. But that puts another set of clouds over an already stormy relationship. I hate thinking of myself as a fickle person, but maybe I am. And not just about guys. It's everything. When I get up in the morning, I'm not at all sure if I'm going to feel happy that day, or sad. I think a lot of the other girls feel the same. Especially the juniors. I think maybe it's like a junior year flu. Why should you be immune?"

Faith nodded, thinking this over, then said, "Even if I really liked Sheff a whole lot, I've already got a boyfriend. Johnny really loves me and I love him. I shouldn't be fooling around with someone else."

It was Dana's turn to think seriously.

"Same with me," she said. "I want to make a big play for Terry, but I really should let go of Randy if I'm going after someone else. But I can't seem to do that. I'm not sure why not. Maybe I'm too scared to be without a boyfriend."

CHAPTER ELEVEN

Roses are red.
Violets are blue.
I'd like to go
For a pizza with you.

Dana wrote this with her calligraphy marker on her good, cream-colored stationery, then folded the sheet and slipped it into an envelope marked, A REALLY TERRIBLE POEM FOR T. O'SHAUGHNESSY — FROM D. MORRISON. Then she ran downstairs and stuck it in his slot in the mailroom off the lobby.

From there, she dashed off to her Friday classes. She had Spanish and algebra and biology, then lunch, then study hall, then creative writing. By the time she saw him there, he should've gotten the note.

She didn't know how she'd be able to wait out the day. And it crawled by like a tortoise.

In Spanish, their teacher taught them some traditional Spanish folk songs. Everyone else thought this was fun. Ordinarily, Dana probably would've thought it was fun, too, but today she just couldn't get into the spirit of "The Merry Burro."

In algebra, she didn't care what either x or y were.

In biology, she was basically grateful that they were done cutting up worms. Hers had been weird inside — not like anyone else's. Today they were talking about the discoveries they had made in the dissection. Dana felt it was an experience best forgotten.

Lunch was cod sticks and beets and Terry wasn't in the cafeteria.

Study hall was an hour's opportunity to play the Clock Game. Dana closed her eyes. If she opened them and the second hand was on an even number, Terry would want to go for pizza with her tonight. If it was on an odd number, he wouldn't. By the end of the hour, the score was 278 to 234 that he would want to go.

And so she sailed into creative writing. The classroom was half full when she got there. Terry hadn't come in yet. Maybe he was dead, she thought. Maybe he had been run over by a car when he was out running this morning and that's why he hadn't been at lunch either.

She stopped herself. She realized she had

slipped into what Faith called "lunatic think-ing." Lunatic thinking was when you zoomed right over all the perfectly reasonable reasons for something right out onto the edge and picked the absolutely most unreasonable and wild explanation. Faith and Dana had dis-covered that they both did this all the time.

Just before the bell rang, Terry rushed into the room and slid into the desk next to Dana. He smiled at her like he always did, but didn't say a thing about the poem.

He probably figures there's not enough time before class starts, Dana thought.

But then class started and when it ended, Terry waited for Dana to gather up her books and walked her out. When they were stand-ing outside, in the beautiful spring afternoon, a perfect moment and place for him to bring up the poem, he told her he had to rush over to soccer practice.

"It looks like they *are* going to let me on the team," he called back to her as he ran off, "as student coach."

She stood there stunned for a moment, then figured it out.

He didn't get his mail yet! she thought.

To assure herself, she walked back over to Baker and into the mailroom to take a peek into his pigeon hole and make sure the cream-colored envelope was still sitting there.

It wasn't!

She couldn't believe it. The poem had been stolen by an international ring of mail thieves.

No. That was lunatic thinking, for sure. More likely, he had gotten the poem and been made shy by the invitation. One of the tough things about being a modern, independent girl, Dana thought, was that some boys were still lagging a little behind the times, and got nervous when a girl asked them out.

She'd just have to lie in wait and ambush him when he got back to the dorm. She could put the meantime to good use in the study lounge, making up conjunction flash-cards for Spanish. Conjunctions were her biggest weak spot. She couldn't keep them straight.

Walking down the hall to the lounge, she almost ran head-on into Casey, who was walking with Keith. Dana smiled. It was so funny seeing Casey walk with him. Keith was a few inches shorter and Casey did this amazing slouch to try to make it look as if they were the same height. What it actually looked like was that she was taller, but had a bad crick in her neck.

Dana smiled and said hi and went into the study lounge. She was the only one in there. It was still pretty early in the term for most of the girls to be hitting the books on Friday afternoon.

She hadn't been there five minutes when Casey came in, alone this time.

"Hi," she whispered to Dana. "Can you talk for a minute?"

"Sure," Dana said. "But I don't think we have to whisper. We're like the tree falling in the forest. If no one's here, we're not making noise."

Usually Casey would have laughed at this, but Dana could see there was no lightening her up right now.

"You're not going to believe this," she started out. "I mean I don't even know how to begin to tell you. It's so bizarre they could put it in *Twilight Zone II*."

"You're in love with Keith," Dana said, trying to make it easier for Casey.

Instead she just looked back at Dana as if she were in shock.

"How did you guess?" she said, back to whispering breathlessly.

"Casey, everybody knows."

"They do? How?"

"Case. You're with him almost all the time. And you're always giving him that look."

"What look?"

"Like you're going to just die of happiness from being around him."

"I do *that*? Really? Oh, no. I'm so embarrassed."

"Why be embarrassed?" Dana asked, putting her arm around Casey's shoulders. "Everybody's happy for you."

"They are?" Casey was clearly amazed. "But don't they think he's a nerd? I know they do. I know everyone calls him Milnerd."

"Well," Dana started, then stopped to think how she could phrase this so she wouldn't offend Casey. "Well, Keith *is* sort of a gobbler. The way he dresses and his hair and all. And the way he's such a human encyclopedia, always spouting off facts about everything. But he's so friendly and open and nice it would be hard not to like him. And he's so happy to be here. I guess what I'm saying is that Keith probably *is* a nerd, but he's *our* nerd, and we like him."

"And you know," Casey said, dropping once again into a whisper, "he's not really all that nerdy once you really get to know him."

"No?" Dana said, doubting that Casey's assessment of Keith would bear much resemblance to reality. She had learned through her teenage listening years that friends in love gave the least accurate pictures imaginable of their true loves. Dana had a real feeling that Casey was pretty much into this stage of making Keith a heroic figure.

"He has such beautiful hands," she was saying.

"I've never noticed his hands," Dana said,

"I'm always too busy looking at his elbows. They're so gorgeous."

Casey didn't pick up on this teasing.

"You think so?" she asked Dana earnestly. "Gee, I hadn't even focused on his elbows yet. I'll have to notice next time."

Dana let this slide. Clearly Casey just needed someone to sit and listen while she shifted into rapture gear for a while.

"He's so wise, Dana. And in so many ways. Like, well, before him, I never really understood the difference between direct and alternating current. . . ."

Casey went on in this vein for about twenty more minutes while Dana sat there, nodding and trying to remember the days when she wished Casey would stop being so disparaging and sarcastic about boys, all those times when Dana couldn't wait for Casey to get a boyfriend of her own. Now here she was, thinking she'd give a week's allowance to hear Casey make just one wisecrack. Who would have thought that when Casey fell in love, she'd be the gooniest and gushiest of them all?

"And then he told me it kind of depressed him that eventually daylight savings time would come around," Casey was saying now. "He says it'll mean losing one of the hours he could spend with me this spring. . . ."

"Uh, Case," Dana interrupted, "I'd just love to hang out and hear lots more about Keith. I mean I had no idea he was such a deep and interesting person. But I've got to get going."

"Oh," Casey said, miffed at being stopped in the middle of her monologue.

"Yeah, I've got a lion trap set for Terry O'Shaughnessy and I've got to go hold the rope to pull it as he runs over the pit."

Casey looked blank. It was clearly too much for her to make the switch from thinking about Keith to thinking about anything else.

"I asked him out this morning," Dana explained. "By note. He hasn't answered. Shy guy is my guess. So I'm going to put myself in his way when he comes in from soccer practice."

"He doesn't *seem* shy," Casey said.

After Dana had left the study lounge and was heading for the lobby, she thought that Casey had a point. Terry did not seem shy. And yet what else could account for his not answering her poem? She was sure he liked her. They talked practically every day. They had practically identical senses of humor. He really seemed to respect what she said about his writing. They were tough, but kind critics of each other's work and had gotten comfortable at showing their writing back and forth. If there was a problem, she couldn't figure out what it was.

She hung out in the lobby for half an hour or so, feeling outrageously stupid. There was no place to wait, really. That's what the main lounge was for. But if she went in there and sat down, Dana knew she'd miss him. No, what she had to do was stand there, leaning against the doorway to the mailroom, trying to look nonchalant as practically everyone she knew came either in or out.

"Hi, Dana. What're you waiting for?"

"Hi, Dana. What's wrong?"

"Hi, Dana. Lost your way?"

"Hi, Dana. Forget whether you were going in or out?"

She could have died of embarrassment. Finally, though, after practically everyone else at Canby Hall had come through those doors, there he was. Unfortunately for Dana, he was in the middle of half a dozen girls from the soccer team. All of them were in sweat pants and jackets and were still goofing around with the ball, kicking it back and forth and laughing at some apparently hilarious incident that had happened out on the playing field.

Why hadn't she thought of this possibility — that he might not come through those doors all alone and ready to talk with her?

Argh, Dana thought, *and here I am, standing around like a total dope. He's going to know I'm waiting for him.*

She tried to make herself look as much

like woodwork as she could. It didn't work.

"Hi, Dana!" he shouted as he passed by her, smiling and friendly as could be. Then, just as he and the girls were about to head around the corner into the machine room to get some Cokes and candy, he looked back at Dana and said, "I loved the poem."

That was it. That was all. Nothing about yes or no or pizza or date. Nothing. And he was gone before Dana had a chance to figure out that this was all he was going to say.

Was it possible that he really thought it was a for-real poem and that she had given it to him to judge its literary merits? Oh, no! Now she was doubly embarrassed. She headed up the four flights to her room as fast as her legs could carry her.

When she got to 407, neither Faith nor Shelley were around, which was good as far as Dana was concerned. She didn't want to talk to anybody about this whole Terry mess until she'd had time to think it through by herself.

She threw herself headlong onto her floor bed, pulled the comforter over her long, rangy body, and shoved her head underneath her pillow.

No sooner had she gotten herself into this position — which she called her "seclusion module" — than she heard someone calling her in the distance.

She lifted the pillow off and turned to see who it was and what they wanted. It was Marilyn McCann, a senior who lived in Baker House.

"Dana!" she said, her head sticking through the doorway. "Phone for you. Randy."

"Will you tell him I got a seat on the first commercial flight to Mars? Tell him I'll be back in about ten light years and I'll give him a call then."

"How about if I just tell him you're not here?" Marilyn said, a little impatient. She lived downstairs at the end of the hall by the pay phone and wound up doing a lot of answering — and lying — for girls on the floor.

"Someday," she threatened, "I'm going to tell the whole truth to every guy who calls. Shake up the old romantic scorecard around this place." It was just talk. Marilyn might be grumpy, but she could be trusted.

When she'd gone, Dana dug herself back into her seclusion module and thought, *Why is it that striking out with a new guy is making me mad at an old guy?*

She knew that if she was going to be upset, it should be at herself, or at Terry. Instead, unreasonably, she was mad at Randy.

She knew he'd be hurt to find her out on a Friday night. Her first thought was, *Serves him right*. Her second thought, though, was *Why does it serve him right? What has he*

*done to deserve me hiding out from him on
a date night?*

And then she knew the answer. It just took
her a little while before she could say it to
herself in her head.

Randy's big crime was that he wasn't Terry
O'Shaughnessy.

CHAPTER TWELVE

Faith was doing a little lying herself that night. Johnny had a part-time job ushering at the Rialto Theater in town. Most Friday nights, Faith went over and stayed through the double feature while he took tickets and told loud kids to pipe down and helped people find umbrellas they'd lost under the seats. Stuff like that. Then, when he was done, they'd go out for bacon cheeseburgers, their favorite food.

Tonight, though, she begged off, saying she had a sore throat and just wanted to crawl into bed with some tea and honey and a big historical romance novel.

But there was not really any sore throat, any tea, or any novel. What there was, was two hours of changing clothes in front of the mirror to find the perfect outfit. A half hour of putting on eye makeup. A talk with Dana about whether ties looked cool on girls, or just weird. And then, at seven-thirty, a dash over to the gym, where Canby Hall and Oakley Prep, the boys school down the road, were having their spring mixer.

Faith tried to talk Dana into coming along with her, but Dana was depressed about Randy calling and Terry not calling, and just wanted to wallow alone in her misery for the rest of the night.

The roommates of 407 had a pact allowing each other one day of brooding over something. After that, the other two could jump in to try and pull the misery-wallower out before she slipped into major depression. They decided this after the time last year when Bret Harper broke up with Dana and she spent the next three days in bed living on taco chips and diet orange soda.

But tonight was Dana's allowed night of despair, and so Faith left her to it and set out across campus alone. She was feeling both guilty and excited at the same time. Guilty over lying to Johnny. Excited at the prospect of dancing in the dark with Sheff.

The outfit she had ultimately decided on was black slacks and a white silk spaghetti strap camisole, set off by glittering eyeshadow. To top it all off, she had borrowed from Dana a vintage black satin tuxedo jacket. She might not look like the female singers Sheff idolized, but she knew that she looked less like a schoolgirl tonight than she ever had. More like a sophisticated young woman with an air of mystery about her.

All this effect might be a total waste. Faith wasn't even sure Sheff was going to be at the mixer. She had asked Casey to ask Keith, who had sent back the Keith-like message, "There is a fifty-three percent probability of Sheff going to the mixer."

Faith knew with one hundred percent probability that Johnny Bates would *not* be at the mixer. In the first place, he was working. In the second place, he thought Faith was sick in bed and wouldn't see the point in going to a dance without her. (This was the kind of thing about him that made her feel so guilty she couldn't stand it.) In the third place, Johnny couldn't stand Oakley Prep boys and was beginning to feel the same way about Canby Hall boys. He wouldn't be caught dead at a mixer with any of them. So, whatever happened tonight, at least Faith was sure she wouldn't get caught at it.

When she got to the gym, she did a quick scan of the room. She noticed almost nothing. Not the pink and green crepe paper streamers taped to the walls. Not the fake apple tree with pink Kleenex blossoms next to the refreshment table. Not the refreshment table. Not Tom and Shelley sitting on the bleachers,

holding hands. Not even Pamela Young, trying to impress everyone by wearing a sequin
top and black leather pants.

To be precise, if a big murder was com-
mitted at this mixer, and the police ques-
tioned Faith afterward as a witness, she would
not be able to tell them a thing except that
Sheffield Adams was there.

When she came in, he was standing in a
corner, talking with Terry O'Shaughnessy.
He was wearing a cream-colored suit and a
black shirt, open at the throat. Nobody
dressed like this for mixers. The rest of the
guys were wearing jeans and crewnecks and
looked like all they'd done in preparation for
the dance was to change their socks. Faith
suspected the average mixer getting-ready
time was two hours for girls, three and a half
minutes for boys.

If Sheff felt out of place for looking so
different from the other guys, he didn't show
it. He probably thought he was cooler than
everyone else, Faith decided. *Of course, he is,*
she thought. Although she wasn't about to
let him see how she felt.

In fact, she wouldn't even let him know
that she saw him. She ignored him as though
he were invisible. She talked with everyone
she knew, danced with every guy who asked
her and then, on a Ladies' Choice slow dance,
walked right up to him and Terry, and asked
Terry to dance with her.

Midway through this number, Sheff walked over and cut in on them.

"If I may," he said, bowing at Terry as he took Faith's left hand, placed it on his shoulder and spun them into motion.

When they'd been dancing a few moments, he said, into her ear, "You're really knocking out the guys here tonight."

"I am?" Faith said, truly surprised. "I didn't notice."

"The question is," he said, pulling away to look questioningly into her eyes, "who in particular are you *trying* to knock out?" He added a sly smile to the end of the question to show that he *knew* who.

"Not you, if that's what you're thinking," Faith said, hoping to wipe that grin off his face.

"No? Then why were you working so hard at ignoring me?"

"Maybe I just didn't notice you."

"Possible," he said, nodding to himself, considering this. "But not likely. I'm pretty noticeable in this setting, and tonight I dressed up especially to get noticed by you."

"You did?"

"Mmmhmm. I'd hate to think it went to waste."

He pulled her back into his arms and whirled them around the floor with some moves that were fancier than any Faith knew from dances back in Washington.

When the slow song ended, he took her hand and led her off the floor.

"I hate disco," he said.

"Me, too," Faith agreed. "It's like the elevator music of rock and roll."

He smiled at her.

"You and I have an affinity," he said, now serious.

"How so?" she asked.

"Deep down inside, we have the same soul prints."

"Oh, my," Faith said, suddenly finding herself without a thing to say back.

"What about if we take a walk?" he said.

She looked at him questioningly.

"Just a short walk," he assured her. "I'd just like to spend five minutes with you without three hundred kids around."

"Okay," Faith said, and followed him out of the gym. Her attention was so focused on him that she didn't notice the small scene going on in the hallway. She didn't see Tom and Shelley by the pay phone.

"Tom," Shelley was saying, "please don't. This isn't your business."

"We Greenleaf High guys have to stick together against this Canby Hall Menace. If we don't help each other, these guys are just going to ooze in and steal our girlfriends, like *Invasion of the Body Snatchers*."

Shelley tried to wrest the quarter from

between Tom's thumb and fingers, but he was too fast and she wound up standing helplessly by while he punched the number of the Rialto and asked for Johnny Bates. Shelley just glared silently at Tom while he waited for Johnny to come to the phone.

"Johnny. Tom. Better get over to this mixer fast. There's a Body Snatcher after your girlfriend. What? I don't know anything about a sore throat. Maybe this guy's her new doctor, but I'm telling you, I don't like the looks of his treatment."

Outside, Faith and Sheff fell under the spell of the soft late winter night. Here in the New England woods, the scents of pine trees filled the air. They both noticed it.

"Smells are like music to me," Sheff said. "Tonight for instance smells to me like a cool clarinet riff. You know what I mean?"

"Mmmhmm," Faith said, although she didn't really see much connection between how maple trees smelled and how a clarinet sounded.

"I knew you'd understand," he said. "You're different from everybody else around here. You're a very hip lady."

Faith smiled shyly at the compliment.

"Yeah," he went on, "we'll have to split from this place some night. After everyone here in Preppyland is asleep. We can hitch into Boston and hit a few of the clubs and discos. I sometimes jam with the musicians there and so I can get us in."

Faith had a hard time imagining herself leaving Canby Hall in the middle of the night to hitchhike all the way to Boston and then spend the night in clubs, but she found herself just nodding at the suggestion.

"You must have some great music places in D.C.," Sheff said.

"Oh, yeah," Faith bluffed, quickly inventing a few night spots. "There's the Blue Note. And Neon — that's *the* dance club."

"It's so easy talking to you," he said. "I like you a lot, Faith. But I need to know, how tied up are you with the baseball player?"

All Faith's guilt came tumbling in around her.

"Pretty tied up," she said. "We've been going together since last year."

"But you did come here tonight looking for me?"

"Oh, Sheff, I'm so confused."

"I'd better take advantage of that, then," he said, and leaned in to give her what she later replayed in her head as the best single kiss of her life (so far).

"We'd better get back," Faith said, a little unsettled by the unexpectedness and wonderfulness of the kiss. She took his hand and led him back up the path toward the gym.

As they approached they could see in silhouette against the bright lights inside, standing like a sentry on the steps, a solitary figure. Too late, Faith saw that the figure was Johnny. There was no way to back off or take another path. All she could do was stand silent before him. There was nothing she could say.

And then it happened, so suddenly she wasn't prepared for it. Neither was Sheff apparently. When Johnny leaped down the steps and slugged a hard right into Sheff's jaw, Sheff just went down like a sack of marbles.

He got up, though, rubbing his jaw. Johnny was dancing lightly in front of him, his fists up, ready for more.

"I can see you've got a big fight in mind here," Sheff told him, "but man, that's just not my style. And besides, there's no point to it. Punching each other around would make this seem like a contest, with Faith as the prize. But she's *not* our prize. She's her own woman. If there is a contest here, the winner's going to be decided by *her* heart, not *our* fists. Now if you'll all excuse me, I'm going to walk my jaw home."

Left alone, facing each other in the moonlight, Faith and Johnny were caught in their own silences. Faith's was one of remorse, Johnny's one of anger. She was the one who finally said something.

"It was me you should have slugged," she said in a voice so soft it was almost a whisper.

"No," Johnny said, "I shouldn't have hit anybody. But I needed to and that creep just happened to be in the wrong place at the wrong time. Give him my most sincere apologies, won't you?" he said as he brushed past her and broke into a run off campus, toward town.

When Faith came through the door of 407, Dana had come out of her depression enough to look up and ask, "So? Was it a fun mixer?"

At which point, Faith fell onto her bed and began sobbing.

CHAPTER THIRTEEN

Dear Jeff:

Whatever's going on at Iowa State, it's got to be calmer than the latest at Canby Hall. Sometimes I look forward to college as a place where I'll be able to recuperate from high school.

My classes are really hard this year. They work juniors to death here. Papers and studying for quizzes keep me too busy to get anywhere near enough time for the really important things in life, like play practice (we're doing a great old comedy this term — *My Sister Eileen*) and going out with Tom, who really does light up my life, even though I know that's an impossibly corny thing to say.

The other two-thirds of 407 are in such deep trouble with males, though, that some adolescent psychologist could come and hang out in our room for a week and go away with enough material for a new textbook.

The root of this problem is that the administration here decided to let in boys. Just three, but it's turned out to be plenty enough. It's as if they let loose a mountain lion, a skunk, and a porcupine for all the problems they've caused.

Well, it's not really them, it's just their being here that's been so disruptive. Dana has fallen for one, Faith for another, Casey for the third. In Casey's case, this is fine and dandy as she was on the loose to begin with. But, as you may remember, both Faith and Dana already have boyfriends on the scene.

I don't know what they're going to do about their dilemmas. They sit around the room all the time wrestling with possible solutions. They ask the Tarot cards. They consult horoscope magazines. They're even planning to go tonight to a fortune-teller who operates out of a trailer on the outskirts of town. I told them they ought to just spend the ten dollars on a good Chinese dinner at Wong's and go with whatever their fortune cookies say.

How are your business courses going? You're not really going to pledge a fraternity, are you? You just seem like too much of an individualist to me for all that.

Oh, yes, I almost forgot. Count me in on the hot dog stand idea. There's really no place downtown for anyone to get a bite to eat except for Dinah's Lunch, which has been killing people slowly for years. A hot dog wagon by the town hall is bound to make us at least millionaires by fall.

I wish you'd come out here sometime. Maybe since you get out earlier for summer break than I do, you can drive out and fetch me.

I've got to go now. We have to go to dinner early so the two disturbed ones here can get to Madame Irene's by six.

Bunches of love,
Shelley (Slugger)

CHAPTER FOURTEEN

After being almost springlike for several days, the weather took a sudden turn on Tuesday. The sun slipped behind angry-looking clouds and the temperature dropped twenty degrees. Faith and Dana had to get out their down jackets and warm gloves for the walk into Greenleaf and beyond, to visit Madame Irene, the fortune-teller.

Every week, Dana had seen the ad in the Greenleaf paper:

MADAME IRENE
SEES THE FUTURE
ANSWERS ALL QUESTIONS ON
HEALTH
MONEY
LOVE
Consultation by Appointment Only. Call . . .

And then there was a phone number. Which

Dana called on Monday, after a long, dismal weekend of not hearing from Terry and wondering what to do about Randy.

After chorale practice, she went down to the basement of the chapel to use the pay phone there. She didn't want anyone to overhear this call.

It rang three times on the other end before someone picked up and said, in a deep, severe voice, "Yes?"

"Madame Irene?" Dana asked.

"Yes."

"Uh, you don't know me, but, uh, I go to Canby Hall, and uh . . ."

"Ah, yes," the voice said, "I zee many girls from zee school. I haf parted zee veils of zee vuture for zeez girls for many years. Many interesting vutures." The voice had a heavy European accent.

"The ad says you answer questions on money, health, and love," Dana said.

The voice laughed heartily and said, "Yes, but eet eez not health or money you vant to ask Madame Irene about, eez eet?"

"Uh, well, no," Dana stammered.

"Come tomorrow. At seex. Breeng ten dollars. No credit cards," she said brusquely, then gave Dana an address and hung up without saying good-bye.

Dana stood looking at the dead receiver for a moment, wondering if this odd conversation had actually taken place.

* * *

As soon as she got back to 407, she began trying to talk Faith into coming along with her, to get Madame Irene to look into *her* future and see if it held Sheff or Johnny.

"How much does it cost?" was Faith's question.

"Ten dollars."

"Oh, boy," Faith said, whistling. "That's a lot. That's half a sweater. That's a large pizza with everything. That's two movies."

"Ten dollars for the answers to your love questions," Dana tempted.

"What makes you think this Madame Irene has these answers? How do you know she can really see into the future?"

"You didn't talk to her. I did. I can tell that she *knows*."

For a long moment Faith just stood there across the room, looking at Dana. Finally, grabbing her books to go down to the study lounge, she said as she passed Dana on her way out, "Okay, I'll come along."

The address Madame Irene had given Dana was in a ramshackle trailer park, filled with dilapidated old mobile homes, their pastel colors faded like overwashed jeans. Dana and Faith were chilled to the bone by the time they got there, and then on top of it all, got nervous when they were in front of Madame

Irene's trailer — an ancient, rounded, pink model.

"We don't have to go in," Dana said as they stood outside the trailer, looking at the warm glow of light coming from within.

"You told her you'd be here," Faith said. "I think we have to keep the appointment."

They walked up the three weatherbeaten wood steps and Dana knocked timidly on the door. They could hear the sound of gypsy music from within.

The door opened and there stood Madame Irene. She was very old, and very tall — taller than either Faith or Dana, who were pretty tall themselves. She was dressed in an amazing number of shawls and skirts and draped in beads and bracelets. She had five earrings dangling from one ear, none in the other. She had a bandanna on her head and was wearing sunglasses, even though it was dusk of a dreary day. She extended an arm out the opened door, crooked a long, ruby-painted fingernail, and beckoned them in without saying a word.

Inside, the trailer was hung with heavy red velvet drapes and charts of the stars. The lighting was dim, coming from an old fringed Victorian lamp on a table in the corner. A huge, gold, velvet couch took up all of one wall. Facing it was a rattan chair with a high, peacock back. Between the couch and the chair was an ornate table of dark wood, its top highly polished.

"Please," Madame Irene said, indicating with a wave of her ring-encrusted hand that they were to sit on the couch.

Dana looked around. The parlor seemed to take up the whole trailer. Did Madame Irene live here? Did she roll back all this velvet and incense and shut off the tape of gypsy violins, and there was a TV set and a microwave? Or was this just her office, like those trailer banks in shopping centers?

"So," Madame Irene said, breaking into Dana's reverie. "Which of you vants fortune told?"

She looked from Faith to Dana and back again, her dark eyes penetrating, her hawk-like nose twitching slightly, her smile revealing a front tooth of gold set with a small ruby.

"Well, actually," Dana said, "both of us. But I can go first."

"All right," Madame Irene said, rearranging her many shawls around her shoulders. "Do you weesh me to read your palm, zee cards? Perhaps zee creestall ball? Zee tea leaves?"

Dana wasn't prepared for these questions.

"Uh, I don't know. What do *you* think?"

Madame Irene fixed Dana with a stare even more intense than before and said, "For you, I think zee palm," she said. "But first, you must cross *my* palm with zilver."

Dana became flustered.

"Oh, my, I didn't know. I didn't bring any silver."

Faith nudged her with a swift elbow.

"She means the ten bucks."

"Oh. Oh, yes," Dana said, standing up to get the ten-dollar bill out of her back jeans pocket. "Here," she said, putting it on the table between them.

"No, my child. You must cross my palm with eet."

Dana picked up the bill and placed it in the open palm of Madame Irene, who — with a motion nearly faster than the speed of light — put it in a little leather box set on the edge of the table.

"Now," Madame Irene said, "give me your palm."

Dana did, and watched as Madame Irene held it and looked at it as if it were a particularly difficult road map. During this period of silence, Dana felt Faith's shoe pressing on her toe. She looked over as much as she could without turning her head, and saw Faith roll her eyes. Clearly she was getting skeptical of Madame Irene. Dana began to be sorry she had talked Faith into coming along. What if this turned out to be really stupid? If it was, she made up her mind, she'd find a way to give Faith her ten dollars back.

Suddenly Madame Irene spoke.

"First I look into zee past. You have a

happy childhood. A sister you love. But then, there eez a sad somezing just back here." She pointed with the tip of her long index finger-nail to a particular spot on Dana's palm. "One of your parents gone away."

"My dad," Dana said, trying to see where Madame Irene was seeing this.

"Yes. He eez gone from zee home, but not from your life. He eez very important to you in zee future. Ah, and you are arteestic, I zee, maybe vis zee music?" she said, smiling her gold-edged smile.

"Yes," Dana said, amazed. "I sing and play the guitar."

"And you chog," Madame Irene went on.

"Pardon?" Dana said.

"*Chog*," Madame Irene repeated. "You run."

"Oh, yes," Dana said. "And that's in my palm, too?"

"No," Madame Irene said, as if Dana were being silly. "I zee your Nike shoes. I think of getting pair myself."

At this, Dana felt Faith shaking next to her with suppressed laughter. Madame Irene didn't seem to notice. She was too intent on Dana's hand.

"So," she went on, "zee boys, zee heart. This eez what you came for, no?"

"Well, yes," Dana said shyly.

"I zee boy."

"Is he blond?" Dana asked.

"Yes," Madame Irene said.

"That's Randy. Do you see anyone else in there? Anyone with dark hair?"

Madame Irene looked at Dana's hand for a long moment.

"Here, many years down the love line, there is a dark-haired man. But not now."

Dana was perplexed. Why wasn't Terry showing up on her love line?

"Do you see anything else?" she asked.

"I zee a move," Madame Irene said. "Not a vacation. Another school."

"College?" Dana asked.

"Yes. Much happiness there."

"What about after?" Dana prodded.

"I zee love and work and children and many dogs."

"Dogs?!" Dana said. She had never had a dog in her life. She wanted Madame Irene to pursue this a little further, but clearly the reading was over. She had let go of Dana's hand and was shifting her attention to Faith, who was wasting no time crossing Madame's palm with her own silver.

"I'd like you to do mine with the crystal ball, though," Faith said.

Madame Irene got slowly out of her chair and went over to a black lacquer cabinet in the corner and pulled from within a small crystal ball and a base made of ebony. She set them on the table between her and Faith.

"Please put your hands flat on zee table,"

she told Faith. "I need you should have connection here."

Faith did as she was asked, and Madame Irene peered deep into the ball. After a short while she looked up at Faith and said, "You, too, have some sadness in your past."

Tears welled up in Faith's eyes as she thought of her dad, a police officer, who had been shot in the line of duty several years earlier.

"You, too, are arteestic, I see," Madame went on quickly.

"I'm a photographer," Faith said.

"Ah, yes," Madame said, nodding. "Sometimes zee ball clouds up a leetle. Ah, this eez interesting. You have already taken a peecture of zee person you will marry."

"I have?" Faith said, unsettled. She had taken hundreds of pictures of Johnny by now, a couple of Sheff.

"Yes," Madame Irene said, "but you have not met heem yet."

This stopped Faith in her tracks. How could this be? But of course, it could. She took pictures everywhere. In Washington. Down in Florida, she took four rolls on the beach alone. And somebody in one of those pictures, someone she didn't know yet, was going to be the guy she married. It was too weird to think about for long. And it meant that — if Madame were right — she wasn't going to marry either Sheff *or* Johnny.

"Madame Irene," Faith said. "What about the present? Can you see my problem in the crystal ball?"

"Yes," Madame said, nodding, then looking up at Faith. "Your answer is, I think, een Shakespeare. To zine own zelf be true."

Faith turned to Dana with a bewildered look.

"To thine own self be true," Dana translated.

Faith nodded and looked down at her purple painted fingernails and then put a hand up to touch the new relaxed curls on her head from the treatment she'd given herself last week. Both felt a little weird and not very *her*. She had been thinking she'd eventually get used to this new image of herself she'd been designing for Sheff, but now she wondered. Maybe Madame Irene was right.

CHAPTER FIFTEEN

Dana waited a few days, thinking over what Madame Irene had said. She didn't want to act on impulse, especially where someone else's feelings were so involved.

By Saturday, though, she knew that to be honest with herself, and with Randy, she had to break up with him. She didn't feel about him the way he felt about her. And she didn't feel about him the way she felt about Terry. It wasn't fair to keep Randy hanging around just to have a boyfriend.

Plus, she suspected that the reason Terry was holding himself so aloof from her lately was that he didn't want to start something serious with a girl who already had a boyfriend.

She woke up early that morning with a start, and got ready without waking up Faith or Shelley. She was afraid that if she started talking with them about it, she would lose her nerve. She just wanted to do it, before she had time to talk herself out of it.

She put on her running shoes and a sweatsuit and headed out through the foggy dawn, past town, past the trailer court where Madame Irene lived, until she got to Randy's family's horse ranch and orchard.

Although it was pretty early in the day to visit most people, she knew the Crowells would be up. Sometimes they were all out and about before their rooster crowed.

She was winded by the time she came through the pasture that fronted their huge, sprawling house, which had been added onto by generations of Crowells. They were one of the oldest landowning families in this part of Connecticut.

Catching her breath, Dana walked the rest of the way around the house to the kitchen door, which stood open. Through the screen came the sounds and smells of breakfast at the Crowells. Sausage splattering and eggs frying and toast toasting. The rich perfume of coffee brewing. The shouts and laughter of all the Crowell boys and their parents. It was so warm and friendly — like it always was around here — that Dana had a brief lapse in her resolve to break up with Randy this morning. If she lost him, she'd lose his great family, too — her family away from home.

It made her really sad to think of never coming out here again.

Caught in these thoughts, she stood at the screen door without knocking. Suddenly, though, someone was shouting her name from inside.

"Hey, Danabanana!"

It was Randy's little brother Eb (short for Ebenezer, an old family name he got stuck with).

And then Randy's mother was pushing the door open with one hand, a spatula in the other.

"Come on in, Dana honey," she said, and so there was nothing Dana could do but accept the invitation. Inside, everyone was happy to see her. They didn't act as if there was anything weird about her being out here at seven in the morning, unannounced and uninvited. They clearly thought of it as a happy surprise.

Before she could stop them, they were pulling up a chair for her and stacking a plate with eggs and sausage and hash browns and toast from Mrs. Crowell's home-baked bread. Through all this, Dana was looking around in confusion.

"Where's Randy?" she was finally able to get in edgewise. He was nowhere to be seen.

"Oh," Mr. Crowell said, "he's gone out to check up on that new foal of Miss Rosie's. Why don't you give him a surprise after you've finished your breakfast? Jamie can saddle up Lumpy for you."

Dana had to smile. The first time she had ridden with Randy, when he was teaching her how, he'd given her Lumpy, the fattest, oldest, slowest horse on the ranch.

"It's as close as we can get to your previous mount," he had teased. She had told him that her only other time on a horse was atop the mechanical Lil Buckeroo out front of the supermarket by their apartment. These rides had cost a quarter and had taken place when she was five.

Now that she had been riding with Randy for several months, she knew she could handle a more spirited horse, but she had come to love gentle Lumpy. And she had no fantasies of riding with the wind like Randy. She figured that for a city girl, it was thrilling enough just to be able to stay on top of a horse, even one moving at a mile per hour.

And so, after breakfast, riding slowly out across the foothills on the back of Lumpy, who moved like a sprung rocker, Dana fell into fond thoughts of Randy, and highlights of their romance.

The time he made her a cake all by himself, for her birthday — completely lopsided with blue and yellow frosting.

The night they drove to the shore and cooked lobsters over a fire on the beach.

The day they sat amid all the wild flowers

on his favorite ridge and read to each other their favorite parts from their favorite books.

She stopped herself. This wasn't going to do any good. The fact was that they hadn't had one of these magic moments in months. And they weren't going to come back.

She tried to get her mind steeled for the conversation she was about to have with him. She tried to imagine what she would say, then what he would say. In her imagination, she was reasonable, but firm. He was hurt, but understanding. According to her script, it was going to go pretty easily, and they would part friends. She tried to have him saying that she should still come out for Sunday dinners with his family, and to bring her new boyfriend if she wanted. But this didn't play and she mentally crossed it out of the script.

Suddenly, she was almost thrown out of her saddle by the loudest clap of thunder she had ever heard. Following close on its heels was a terrifying bolt of lightning that crackled down out of the sky and seemed to strike the ground just the other side of the cluster of trees at the bottom of the hill.

"Holy cow!" Dana shouted, even though she was alone with no one around to hear her. She dug her heels into Lumpy's sides to try to get the old girl going. But this only caused her to increase her speed from one to about two miles per hour. At this rate, Dana would never beat the storm, which she could see approaching, tumbling across the sky blackly. She felt like the melodrama heroine tied to the tracks, watching the locomotive bearing down on her.

She dug her knees into Lumpy.

"Come on, girl!" she shouted, trying to sound like Annie Oakley. But Lumpy just turned her head around and gave Dana a you've-got-to-be-kidding look, snorted wetly, and kept up with what was, for her, high gear.

Then the rain came — a real deluge, heavy drops coming at Dana on the diagonal, pushed by the fast winds. And she had very little protection. The day had come up so nice that she had worn only a jacket over her sweats, which were now thoroughly soaked and stuck to her body.

Just when she was wondering how she was ever going to get out of this — by now the rain was so heavy she couldn't even see where she was going — someone rode up from behind her and grabbed Lumpy's reins, and suddenly she was off and running.

It was Randy, of course, swooping in on her to save the day. Like a Mountie. Or Superman. He took her and Lumpy to an old lean-to, which gave them shelter from the worst of the rain, which passed, like most heavy storms, very quickly.

In its wake came a huge burst of sunshine and something Dana had never seen — a double rainbow, one over the other.

"Wow!" she whispered. The sight took her breath away.

"Like it?" Randy said. "I ordered it special for you. What are you doing out here anyway? I must say I was plenty surprised to run into a damsel in distress out in that storm, but I was triply surprised to find it was you."

"Oh, I was coming out to see you. Your dad said you were looking after Miss Rosie's foal."

He looked at her skeptically.

"It's the first time you've ever come out here just to give me a surprise. You're not usually even awake on Saturdays until noon."

"Well, uh, I wanted to talk and this seemed like a good time and place. I didn't count on the storm. I didn't count on you rescuing me like a hero out of some Western."

"I should've let you drown out there?"

"Well, no," she said.

"Actually, I was trying to save Lumpy. She's a good old horse and we wouldn't want to lose her. You just happened to be on her back and so you got saved as part of the package." When this didn't get a smile out of her, he asked, "Come on, why wouldn't you want me to save you? What's wrong with that? Isn't that what boyfriends are for?"

"Randy," she said, blurting it because she knew if she didn't get it out now, she might never, "the thing is I don't want you to be my boyfriend anymore. Oh, gee, that sounded awful. Let me start over. I like you a lot. You know that. But things have changed between us. You can see this romance is not what it used to be."

"I can see it's not what it used to be before you started growing your own boyfriends right there on campus. You don't need to import them from Greenleaf anymore. Preppies, all together. Townies, get lost. I *get* the picture, Dana. Don't insult me by spelling it out anymore."

She hadn't expected this. Randy blaming this all on Terry was not in the script Dana had written. Neither was his getting up on his horse and taking old Lumpy by the reins, leaving Dana sitting in the lean-to.

"But, Randy!" she wailed. "I'm soaking wet and it's a long way back to school on foot."

He turned in the saddle, looked down on her with contempt and said, "Suffer."

And left her sitting there quite stunned. This was not at all how it should have gone. She hadn't gotten to tell him all the ways he was still important to her. She hadn't gotten even close to proposing they build a warm friendship out of the cold ashes of failed romance. She didn't have a chance to explain all the complex reasons for her leaving.

Actually, if anyone was left, ultimately it

was her. She was, after all, the one sitting in the mud, wet as an overcooked piece of macaroni.

Still, just as there was a double rainbow as a result of the terrible storm, there was, she thought, at least one good result of this awful scene. She could now tell Terry O'-Shaughnessy that she was free and clear of old emotional entanglements, that the two of them could now throw themselves into the romance they'd been holding back from.

With this fantasy filling her head, she hardly noticed how yucky it was walking back through the spring morning with her clothes stuck to her body and the heavy treads of her running shoes making suction sounds with every step she took through the mud.

CHAPTER SIXTEEN

That night — Saturday — the roommates and Casey and the three male members of the Canby Hall student body all wound up together at Pizza Pete's. This dinner was the end result of a series of events that began with a fight and ended with a double surprise.

The fight was between Tom and Shelley, over the phone, late in the afternoon. By then he had gotten word about Dana dumping Randy. In Randy's version, the dumping was one hundred percent about Terry O'Shaughnessy. Just like Faith and Johnny not speaking for the past week was one hundred percent about Sheffield Adams.

"About the only one of those guys I can remotely stand is that nerd," Tom was saying to Shelley. "At least he had the basic sense to go for a girl who didn't already have a perfectly fine boyfriend here in Greenleaf."

111

"You're being unreasonable and you know it," Shelley said. "Nothing's even going on between Dana and Terry. And if Faith wants to leave Johnny, it's not Sheff's fault. It's not like these guys set out lures for us."

"What do you mean *us?*" Tom said suspiciously.

"I mean the generic Canby Hall girls *us*, what do you think I mean?"

"I just wonder why you're grouping yourself in with the others? Are you just hanging in with me until one of the Big Three slots opens up, until you can get a Canby Hall guy of your own?"

At this Shelley looked at the receiver for a moment as if it were an electrical eel, then threw it back into the cradle, giving Tom a momentary earache on the other end, and a pretty good idea of how she had taken the remark.

Shelley's being insulted was the first link in the chain of events that Saturday afternoon, as it left her unusually dateless for that night.

"Hey, Faith," she said, flopping onto Faith's bed next to her.

"Hey!" Faith said, "you're crushing valuable negatives here. Come on. Get up."

Shelley sat up and helped Faith get the negatives out of the way. Then she lay back down again.

"What I was wondering was what you're doing tonight."

"I'm not sure. I was kind of waiting around to see what materialized out of the rubble of my life. I doubt that I'll be hearing from Mr. Bates as I have not heard from him in eight days and nothing's happened in those eight days to make him reconsider."

"Are you officially broken up?"

"I haven't seen them carving it into a plaque on the front of Baker, if that's what you mean."

"Come on," Shelley said, "I'm serious."

"I don't know, Shel. Really. He hasn't called because he's furious with me. Which he has a right to be. I haven't called him because I don't have anything to say that he's going to want to hear. I did send an apology note, but he didn't answer."

"What about Sheff?"

"That's another I-don't-know. I've seen him twice this week and both times were fun, but I don't know. It's not an easy, relaxed kind of fun. It's like I'm performing for him. He seems pleased with the performance. He thinks I'm real witty and sophisticated and mature beyond my years — just like he is. But I'm not so sure. I mean, if I am all those things, how come I'm so tired after a couple of hours of doing that? I mean, girl, it is hard work being with that boy."

"Well, it's hard work being with Tom

these days, too. He thinks I'm going to join the stampede to leave my good old Greenleaf boyfriend and run off with a Boy of Canby Hall."

"I believe they're all taken at the moment," Faith said, rolling off the bed onto the floor, where there was half a Snickers bar, which she unwrapped and ate. "Hmm. Wonder how long this has been around?"

"He thinks I'm standing in line, taking a number," Shelley said. "We had a rather major fight over this on the phone just now."

"So what you're saying is that you're free tonight?"

"Mmmhmm," Shelley said, nodding.

"Dana is, too," Faith said. "She and Casey and Keith were talking about going to the show, but as you might expect, I'm not crazy about turning up at the Rialto."

At that moment, Casey burst into the room, holding a hand up, palm out in the air.

"Hold everything, folks!" she shouted. "We've got what I believe is a culinary milestone tonight. They just put up those horrible little white letters on the black felt board, the ones that warn us of the nightly disaster that is about to occur in the Baker cafeteria. Now, we all know the dire consequences of the word 'surprise' on that board. As in Hawaiian Surprise or Pork Surprise or Tomato Surprise. We all know that the surprise is never a pleasant one. But tonight, the ever-creative kitchen staff has outdone itself with — and you have to believe me, I just now saw it with my own eyes — *Surprise Surprise!*"

First there were groans all around, then a brief silence, then Dana wondering aloud, "I wonder if *anyone* will go down to dinner tonight?"

"Agatha Ambrose," Shelley said. "She loves the food here. She told me."

"She must have come here from a penitentiary then," Faith said. "That's the only place that could make the food here seem okay."

"Well, clearly," Dana said, "we are going to have to go to Plan B."

Plan B was always scraping together everyone's allowance and heading over to Pizza Pete's in town.

"I'll tell the guys," Casey said. "They haven't been here long enough to know the true meaning of the word 'surprise.' I'll see if they want to come with us."

Which was how Dana, Faith, Shelley, Casey, Keith, Terry, and Sheff all wound up an hour later sitting around the big oak table in the back of Pizza Pete's, arguing over whether to get sausage and mushrooms or pepperoni and black olives.

"Few days, no see," Terry said, smiling at Dana, who had accidentally on purpose taken the chair next to him.

"Yeah," she said and sighed. "I had to cut creative writing yesterday so I could cram for a first aid quiz. Can you believe they already want us to be able to give the Heimlich maneuver, mouth-to-mouth resuscitation, plus know how to apply a tourniquet, and treat shock and snakebite."

"They skipped rescuing someone from quicksand?" he said with a twinkle in his eye.

He must like her, she thought, if he teased her like this. He was just shy about actually dating as long as she had another boyfriend. Which she didn't anymore. What she had to do now was find a way to work this information into the conversation.

"Plus I've been busy breaking up with my boyfriend," she said, then stopped in complete astonishment at having said this. Sometimes she felt like a ventriloquist's dummy, like somebody else was putting the words in her mouth. How could she be so obvious, so inept? She tried to think of a way to cover up the blunder, but Terry responded before she could.

"Oh," he said, "I'm sorry. I know that can be rough. I've been through it myself. . . ."

Hmmm, she thought, *so he's broken up with someone before. Maybe that's why he's been a little standoffish. He doesn't want to get hurt again.* So she tried to think of something to say that would be friendly, but not too forward and scary. What she came up with was, "Well, I guess I'm finally going to get that pizza with you."

He shifted around in his seat and looked uncomfortable. She thought maybe he didn't remember.

"The poem," she reminded him.

"Oh, yeah," he said and then paused as if he were groping for the right words. "Well, it's more fun having pizza with a whole bunch of friends, don't you think?"

What planet are you from? was what she thought. What she said, though, was, "Oh, sure. This way we can have a really huge fight over what to order on it."

Faith had been listening in on this exchange. She thought it was pretty likely that Dana was barking up the wrong tree with Terry, and wasn't letting herself see this. She'd approach her about this later, when they were alone. Right now she had to concentrate on the business at hand — ignoring Sheffield Adams, who was sitting across the table from her.

She didn't know why they played these games with each other. They were really his games, but why did she go along with them? This one was "Who's Cooler Than Whom?" The point was to pay as little attention as possible to the other person, to pretend they were a perfect stranger. Especially if you'd just been out with the other person the night before. Double especially if you'd kissed them in the Maple Grove.

Casey and Keith probably never play stupid

games like this, Faith thought, looking across at them. They so clearly got a big charge out of each other, and let it show.

At the moment, Keith had his calculator out and a notepad open on the table. He was trying to persuade the waitress to make up the pizza with mushrooms on three-eights of it, sausage and black olives on one-eighth, and bacon and garlic on the other half.

The waitress' name was Dorothy. She'd worked at Pizza Pete's for so many years that the letters of DOROTHY had almost faded away on her nametag. She'd served pizzas to so many kids that she'd heard everything by now. She listened to Keith, then tapped her pencil against her order pad and said, "That's one large with half mushroom and sausage, half bacon and garlic," and walked away before anyone could correct her.

"They should hire Dorothy at the Baker cafeteria," Dana said.

"Yeah," Sheff responded, "she could make everybody eat Surprise Surprise and like it."

Everybody laughed, and just as they did, three guys pushed open the front door of the restaurant, looked in, and backed right out again.

On the sidewalk, the three of them huddled together.

"Cozy group, eh?" Tom said.

"Yeah," Randy replied. "It warms my heart

to see the boys and girls of Canby Hall out together enjoying themselves."

"Glad I got the night off from work so I could be here to see this," Johnny added.

"Boy, I'd really like to get those guys," Randy said.

"But how?" Johnny asked.

"If only we had a pit of alligators handy," Tom said.

"Or a tank of piranhas," Randy said.

"I know!" shouted Johnny, "what about nuisancing them?"

"What's nuisancing?" Tom asked.

"Oh, you know. Like while they're here having a good time with our girlfriends, we go back and fix their room up real nice. Like the Welcome Wagon."

"Good idea," Randy said. "And I've got a perfect final touch. We do it so they think it was the girls who pulled the stunt."

"Randy," Tom said, patting him on the shoulder. "Sometimes you are positively brilliant."

"Glad you like it," Randy said, smiling. "We'd better hurry, though, if we're going to make this work."

As the three of them headed for Randy's pick-up truck, they passed the window of Pizza Pete's. At that precise moment, no one at the big table in the back was looking up toward the front.

CHAPTER SEVENTEEN

"Well, good-night, ladies," Keith was saying. The whole group was hanging around the front door of Baker, not really wanting to go in, but not being able to think of an excuse to stay out any longer.

"Yes," Sheff said, bowing from the waist, "*Adieux mademoiselles.*"

"*Enchanté,*" Terry added, bending to kiss each of the four girls' hands.

This started everyone laughing.

"That's why we love you guys," Casey said. "Because you're so *continental.*"

"I'm going to put Scotch tape here on my hand where you kissed it," Faith told Terry. "Just like I did when I reached out and touched Michael Jackson's glove as he came out of the stage door that time in Washington."

"Come on, you two," Terry said to his

roommates. "Get me out of here before these girls kill me with sarcasm."

After everyone had made their good-byes, the girls headed through the lobby to go up the main stairway to the fourth floor. The guys headed down the small stairway into the basement. The first clue they had to something being amiss was when Sheff reached out to open the door.

"Hey, come on man," Terry said. "What's the problem?"

Sheff held out a greasy-palmed hand.

"It appears our doorknob has been Criscoed."

The three of them looked at each other for a moment, but nobody had any answers, and so Sheff said, "I guess I'd better go down to the janitor's closet and get some paper towels or we'll never get in."

"That's okay," Keith said, "I've got a handkerchief." And he pulled one from his back pocket.

"Keith," Sheff said, shaking his head in amazement. "You must be the last guy in America to carry a handkerchief."

"My mother says you never can tell when a lady will start crying and need one."

"Especially with you around," Terry teased, taking the kerchief and opening the door with it. It wasn't until the moment they stepped into their room that they realized the extent of the joke that had been played on them.

The room was barely recognizable. It looked like a white cave. Toilet paper was draped over everything — the beds, the desks, the chairs. On the walls, in four-foot-high shaving cream letters was written "HI, GUYS! YOU'RE SO CUTE!"

"What a mess," Terry said, shaking his head.

"It smells weird, too," Keith noticed.

It took them half an hour to find all the hidden, opened cans of sauerkraut and sardines. And then, just when they were done pulling up all the toilet paper and wiping off all the shaving cream, Keith went into their bathroom.

"Oh, no!" he moaned. The other two ran in to find that the tile walls had been smeared with marshmallow, butterscotch, chocolate, and strawberry toppings. On the mirror in bright red lipstick was the message, A BANANA SPLIT FROM 4 SECRET ADMIRERS. Taped to the mirror was a banana.

"I guess we don't have to guess who did all this," Sheff said.

"But they were with us all night," Keith said.

"Not quite," Sheff said. "If you remember, they told us to meet them in the lobby at seven, and we had to cool our heels for a good fifteen minutes before they showed up."

By the time they finished cleaning up the bathroom and headed for bed, it was past one. The three of them were exhausted.

They raced full-tilt into their beds. And each of them was stopped midway.

"Oh, no!" Sheff cried. "We've been short-sheeted!"

"This is the last straw," Terry said, pulling his sheets off the bed and trying to put them down in some rough way that would let him sleep between them.

Sheff was doing the same thing and said, "I think we're going to have to give those girls a dose of their own medicine. If they like pranks, we'll have to show them how the major leaguers work."

Terry smiled and pulled his demolished covers up to his neck. He yawned and said, "Good idea, Sheff. I'll try to get up early tomorrow. That's when the frog catching's best."

"I'll make a run into Boston," Sheff said. "I know where there's a trick store."

"I'll go with you," Keith said. "I hate to do this to Casey, but I have to say those girls really deserve it."

"Let's see," Terry said sleepily. "It's Friday. We'll really need the weekend to get everything together. So what do you say we schedule Operation Revenge for Monday?"

"Fine," Sheff said.

"That's okay by me, too," Keith said. "Let's synchronize our calendars."

The other two sat up to look at him, to see if he was kidding or not. Sometimes with Keith it was hard to tell. Now it was impossible, as he was already asleep.

CHAPTER EIGHTEEN

H ey!" Dana said as she was going through the small wicker basket on her dresser, "did either of you two borrow my feather barrettes?"

"Not me," Faith said.

"Nuh meh," Shelley said in a garbled voice. She was sitting on her bed, putting on her socks. Between sock one and sock two, she fell back onto the bed and went back to sleep.

"Give her a shake, will you?" Dana asked Faith.

"I think she's getting worse, don't you?" Faith said. "I think we really *are* going to have to buy those cymbals." She gave Shelley's shoulder a good shake, and, for good measure, flipped on the radio next to her head and turned the volume up high. This caused Shelley to sit up and open her eyes and begin putting on sock number two, clearly oblivious that she had had any down time between this and sock number one.

Faith had another kind of morning problem. Although she was usually the first one awake in 407, she was always the last to be ready to go down to breakfast. In between getting up and getting out, she just found so many interesting and important things that needed doing. Sorting through negatives. Finishing whatever magazine article she'd fallen asleep reading the night before. Cleaning the lint out of the vent holes in her blow-dryer.

Dana was well aware of this and now stood impatiently, her hands on her hips, looking at her two roommates as if they were pathetic beyond words.

"You two are impossible," she said. "I'm going to go down ahead of you. You know. Just for fun, I'd like to make some of my morning classes."

She opened the door, and in her rush out didn't see the box on the floor until she had kicked it halfway across the hallway.

"What have we got here?" she said, picking it up, turning it over.

It was a square package, maybe four inches on each side, wrapped in bright green foil paper, tied with a purple ribbon. There was a card attached.

"Oooooo, boy!" Dana said, turning back toward the room and reading aloud from the card. "Kisses for the princess of 407, my sweetest Faith."

"It's for me?" Faith said.

"I guess," Dana teased. "I suppose you're the sweetest Faith in the room, by virtue of being the only Faith." Dana handed her the box.

"The card's not signed," Faith said, rereading it for herself.

"Could be a make-up present from Johnny," Shelley said. She now had both shoes on, but had just realized that she had forgotten to put her jeans on first, and would have to start over.

"Not likely," Faith said. "It's more Sheff's style. Actually, it's not really anybody's style, at least anybody I know. But here it is anyway."

Dana, who had been in such a big hurry two minutes before, now came back into the room and sat down at her desk chair.

"So," she prodded Faith. "You going to open it?" Shelley stood up, came over and stood behind Dana, waiting.

Faith looked into the curious stares of her two friends and said, "Uh, if you don't mind, I think I'm just going to open this in the closet."

Privacy was a hard thing to come by at Canby Hall. In 407, if someone really needed to be alone, to think or read a letter or something, the closet was about her only refuge.

Shelley and Dana just stayed where they were and waited while Faith went into the closet, pulling the door mostly shut after her. They could hear her pushing shoes around to make a space, then sitting down. Then they could hear the crinkle of the foil coming off. After that, there was a brief moment of total silence followed by a blood curdling scream.

"Eeeeeeeeeeeeeeeee!!!!" Faith ran full-tilt into the room, dropped the box onto the floor as she went, and sped past Shelley and Dana into the hall.

Shelley and Dana looked at each other for a second, stunned, then looked toward the closet doorway, out of which came hopping a largish, green bullfrog. The two of them, putting the story together in their heads, burst out laughing.

Faith came back into the room. "Yeah, you two think it's funny because it's all the way across the room, and on the floor. Imagine sitting in the dark, thinking that box had something really good in it, and then having that slimy blob spring out at you!"

But they couldn't stop laughing.

"You tough chicks from the inner city," Dana teased when she could get her breath back, "a little froggy sends you to the ceiling."

Faith didn't say anything, just strutted back and forth a little, like a bird whose tail feathers have been ruffled.

When the other two regained their composure, other ramifications of the joke began to crop up in their heads.

"But *whose* joke is this?" Dana asked.

"And why?" Shelley added.

Faith narrowed her eyes.

"You're sure it's not *your* idea of Monday morning fun?" she grilled them.

They both shook their heads fast.

"Not me."

"Not me."

"Then who?" Faith wondered. She was interrupted by the bell gonging out nine o'clock from the Canby Hall chapel.

"Oh, no," Dana said. "That stupid frog made me miss my breakfast!"

"Speaking of which," Shelley said, "where did the little guy go?"

"Oh, no!" Faith said, "and it's first class already so we don't have time to find him. By the time we get back this afternoon, he'll probably have found his way into my bed, or my shower cap, or someplace where he can scare the daylights out of me again. I'll positively kill whoever gave me this *present*."

Later in the day, Dana got a different kind of surprise. In creative writing, Antonia Chase was handing back work from the previous week. She was full of praise.

"I think this is the best lot you've done yet," she said to the class. "With one exception." She picked up a single sheet from the top of the sheaf she was holding and held it aloft between pinched fingers, as if it were something that had gone bad in the back of the refrigerator.

"Dana," she said. "This is not up to your usual work. Frankly, it made me angry. I mean I wonder if this is your idea of a joke." She reread the sheet silently, then — to Dana's humiliation — aloud.

> "Elmer Fudd
> Slips in the mud.
> Falls with a thud.
> Feels like a dud.
> Gets covered with crud."

The whole class went into hysterics. No one was laughing harder than Terry O'Shaughnessy, although he seemed to be trying to hide it behind his hand. What Dana couldn't see was that, laughing even harder out in the hallway were Sheff and Keith.

"Well?" Antonia Chase said, looking at Dana. "Is that what this is — your idea of a joke?"

"I think it's someone else's idea," Dana said. "And I'm going to find out who."

When Dana got back to the room, Faith was there, on her hands and knees, going around saying "ribit, ribit" in a croaky voice. She looked up when Dana came in.

"Hi. I'm trying to make him think there's another frog here, a friendly one he'll want to come out and meet."

"Forget the frog," Dana said. "Things are getting worse." She told Faith about the fake poem someone had substituted for the one she had really written. When she was done, Shelley came wailing into the room, and threw herself onto the bed sobbing. The other two rushed over and eventually got her calmed down enough so that she could tell her story.

"Oh, it was just awful. At rehearsal. I'm playing Eileen. It's this really nice scene between me and my sister. But every time it came to a line of mine, this chicken clucking came over the loudspeakers. Cluck, cluck, cluck, cluck. You know. It was horrible. Someone went to check the sound system, but there wasn't any record or tape playing. Somebody had rigged up something, though; they'd somehow plugged into the speakers so they could run that darned clucking every time I even got close to opening my mouth. You'd think the rest of the cast would have been more sensitive to my dilemma, but they just laughed like loons, then put Theresa Goodman in my place. To see if the clucking would stop. And it did. So they're still rehearsing over there. And I'm here — driven away by some insane cluck."

Dana consoled Shelley with her own story from the creative writing class.

"Boy, somebody's really out to get our goats," Faith said. "But I can't figure out who, or why."

"Maybe it's over now. They've got each of us now," Shelley said. But she was forgetting one important somebody, who at that very moment burst into the room.

"Hey, sports fans!" Casey said. "How's about a little din din?" She got stopped dead in her tracks by the woebegone looks on the faces of the three roommates, and sat down when they began telling her their stories.

"Don't worry," she said when she had heard all the evidence. "We'll catch these jokers. Detective Flint's on the case now with her patented Eagle Eye. Now come on and forget your miseries and let's get downstairs. I hear P.A. has some big wig potential moneybags here today, considering whether or not they're going to give us a new science building or something. They're getting the grand tour, part of which — if you can believe it — is dinner in the Baker cafeteria. Anyway, I figure it means the food has to be at least marginally edible tonight to impress the royalty, so let's go."

Outside the cafeteria, the little white letters on the black felt board spelled out BEEF STROGANOFF under the heading TONIGHT'S ENTREE.

"See," Casey said, "What did I tell you?"

"It's just hamburger in sludge, like half the main courses around here," Faith said. "They've just given it a fancier name because these VIPs are here tonight."

Once they were inside and had their trays on the slide rail and had gotten their salads, jello molds, and rolls, and were just about up to the steam table, there was a commotion behind them.

Patrice Allardyce was coming in with a group of five or six distinguished-looking men and women.

"Apparently she's forgotten her own rule about not cutting in line," Dana whispered to Faith.

Ms. Allardyce and her entourage just kept bustling past everyone already in the line.

"Right this way, please. The girls won't mind," she was telling them as they squeezed past Faith, who was at the end of the line, then Dana, then Shelley, then Casey, who was in front. All this commotion distracted the girls from what was going on behind the steam table. None of them saw Keith Milton, disguised as a kitchen helper, come out and take away a half-full tray of beef stroganoff and replace it with a full one.

This particular tray was not only full of beef stroganoff, but also had a surprise inside. And it was nothing like the fun surprises that come in Crackerjack boxes. This surprise was a very realistic looking rubber hand, positioned so that it was just emerging from the swamp of stroganoff.

The hand was intended to make Casey Flint jump about three feet into the air. But, because of all the jockeying around engineered by Patrice Allardyce, it had this same effect on Mrs. Hortense Wellford, an extremely rich widow from Boston, who at that particular moment had just decided to endow Canby Hall with a new science building.

And it was at that same moment, when Mrs. Wellford screamed a scream that nearly reached high C, and simultaneously threw her tray and the jello mold sitting on it up in the air, that Keith and Sheff and Terry, all of whom had been crouched behind a dish cart in the back of the kitchen, knew that they had gone one joke too far.

CHAPTER NINETEEN

The announcement came directly from Patrice Allardyce, at a special all-school assembly that night at eight in the auditorium. When P.A. called a special assembly, it was hardly ever good news. Tonight it was extremely *bad* news.

Ms. Allardyce had come out onstage with no notes. Whatever she had to say would apparently be short.

"I'm sure that by now you are all aware of the unfortunate incident that occurred in the Baker cafeteria this evening. I am also sure that the comedians who perpetrated the joke will want to come forward and take credit for their lively sense of humor. But just to help them along, I am restricting the entire student body to campus, with no visitors allowed, until the humorists reveal themselves to me and take responsibilty for their action."

And with that she strode off the stage, leaving the whole student body of Canby Hall buzzing.

"Well," Faith said, "for once old Ms. Allardyce has made things easier for us instead of harder." She and Dana and Shelley and Casey were following the crowd up the aisle, out of the auditorium.

"How do you mean?" Casey turned to ask.

"Well, when whoever put the hand in the stroganoff confesses, we've got our gremlin, too. I'm sure it's the same person who played all those other jokes. Even the hand was intended for one of us, I'm pretty sure. I think P.A. and her big wig pals just got in the wrong line at the wrong time."

As they came outside and started down the front steps of the old red brick auditorium building, its front covered in ivy, Dana suddenly found Terry walking by her side. She was surprised. When Antonia Chase had read that stupid poem, he'd laughed harder than anyone in the class. She was hurt that he hadn't taken her side, been her champion. And so she decided to give him a frosty.

"Oh," she said in her most excruciatingly bored tone of voice. "Hi, Terry. What's up?"

"I've got to talk to you, Dana," he whispered, apparently so the others wouldn't hear. "Alone."

She looked over. The look of pain on his

face melted her frosty one completely away.

"Now?" she asked.

He nodded.

"Okay. Let's take a walk. Just sort of around campus."

He nodded again. She had a feeling that if she'd said, "Let's take a walk to the moon," he would've nodded.

"Hey, you all," she said to her friends. "Terry and I are going to split off here." Faith and Shelley and Casey all looked over and gave her their Curious Eyeball looks, but nobody said anything, and so she was able to get away from them without any hassling.

When she and he had gone maybe a hundred feet, she tried to start him off. She was eager to hear what he had to say. She was hoping it would be an apology for laughing at her in class, followed by a declaration of mad love for her. Well, mad *like*, anyway.

Instead, he took her completely by surprise by saying, "We did it."

At first she didn't understand.

"Did what?"

"We put the hand in the stroganoff. Me and Sheff and Keith. All the other stuff, too."

This was much worse than she could have possibly predicted. At first, she couldn't even think of a response. Finally she asked, "But why?"

"To get back at you, of course."

"For *what*?" She couldn't believe her ears. What could he be talking about?

"Well, for tricking out our room like that last night."

"Terry," she said, stopping him with a hand on his arm and turning toward him so she could look him in the eye, "I don't have a clue what you're talking about."

He looked bewildered.

"You know. The toilet paper and shaving cream and the banana split."

She shook her head.

"You didn't do it?" he asked.

She kept shaking her head.

"But all the messages on the walls pointed to it being you. The banana split in the bathroom was from 'four secret admirers.'"

"I'm telling you it wasn't us," Dana insisted. "We wouldn't do something like that even if we really hated you. And why would we hate you? Why would anyone? I can't think of anyone who would hate you guys."

As soon as she said those words, she knew who had sabotaged the guys' room. She told him.

"Our boyfriends."

"Huh?" Terry said.

"Randy and Johnny and Tom. They think you guys are stealing us away from them."

"Why would they think that?" he said.

"Shelley's not interested in any of us and Casey wasn't attached to anyone when she and Keith started going together. Faith, well Faith's going to have to make her own choice. I know Steff would like to be her steady, but ultimately nobody really steals anyone away from anyone else. The person going makes the choice."

Listening to his recitation, Dana noted that he skipped completely over her and him. Maybe he was too shy to mention it directly.

"You're probably wondering why I asked to talk to you about this," he said.

Dana smiled.

"Well, I'm taking it as a good sign."

He seemed to miss this bit of flirtation. He was clearly tied up in a large clump of knots.

"It's that — aside from the guys — you're my best friend around this place, and I really need some advice right now and I'm afraid that since they're involved in this with me, they won't be real objective. The thing is I don't know whether to confess or not. To Ms. Allardyce, I mean."

"Oh, Terry. I think you have to. Someone'll find out and if you don't turn yourselves in, they'll kill you guys. Especially if they've been campused for a while. You haven't seen three hundred girls confined to this place. It's pretty grim. Like *Women of Alcatraz*. I know it's hard, but I think you've just got to do it. And who knows, P.A. might go easy on you. It's happened before." She hesitated. "Once maybe."

"But what if she tosses us out?" he moaned. "I mean the whole reason I came here was so that when Chris comes next year, we can be together again. How am I going to tell her I've been thrown out?"

Dana felt her stomach slide down into her knees. Apparently Chris wasn't his best friend, or his favorite sister, or his cute little Irish setter pup.

In fact, just saying her name seemed to be enough to turn him completely goony.

"You know," he said, "we've known each other since we played in the same sandbox. We've been going together since seventh grade. I know it probably sounds crazy, but I've never even been interested in another girl. I don't think I ever will be. Our big plan was to go all through high school and college together and then get married. Well, that went haywire when my dad got transferred out here. But then I found out about this girls' school that was letting boys in and I figured it was the answer to my prayers. She talked her folks into letting her transfer out here, and I thought we had it made again. Until this stupid mess."

"When I first asked you why you came

here, you pretended you didn't even know it was a girls' school. And you didn't mention a love of your life."

He smiled an embarrassed grin.

"Well, it seemed like kind of a lot of answer to a little question. I thought I'd mentioned Chris to you before. Oh, well, now you know my whole, long, sad story. So what do you think I ought to do?"

Clearly he didn't have any idea what effect his "long, sad story" was having on Dana. Apparently he had never been interested in her. Not like she had wanted, anyway. That's why Madame Irene hadn't been able to see a dark-haired man in Dana's palm. Terry had never been in Dana's life, only in her mind.

She felt like running away and crying. But she knew that was a really childish response. He didn't know how she felt. He never had. He thought of her as a good friend, and now he was in a jam and coming to her for advice. She'd have to be a petulant baby to turn on her heel and stomp off now. And so she stayed and put her hand on his shoulder — buddy to buddy — and said, "You've still got to tell P.A. Believe me, she'll find out anyway. She always does. And it'll be worse for you then. Much better if you come forward yourselves. Then you've got a shot. She has been known, on rare occasions, to actually show mercy. And if she doesn't, we'll help you all we can. No matter how much trouble you are, I know at least the four of us really want to keep you boys at Canby Hall."

When she got back to 407, Shelley was down in the study lounge. Faith was at her desk, working on an essay for her English composition class.

"I figure, as long as we're grounded, I might as well use the time to get out of the hole on my homework," she looked up and told Dana. "I figure I'm about three terms behind now."

"Have you got a minute?" Dana asked. "I hate to interrupt you."

"No, it's okay," Faith said, closing the spiral notebook she'd been writing in. "I was kind of waiting for you to get in. There are a couple of things I've been wanting to talk with you about."

"Okay," Dana smiled, "you first."

"Johnny called," Faith said.

"And?"

"And I apologized for stepping out on him."

"And?" Dana prodded again.

"And I asked him if he'd consider taking back a faithless fool like me."

"You did! But what about Sheff?" Dana pulled her desk chair up close to Faith's and sat down.

"Well, I've been trying all week to think through the situation and I came to the conclusion that if I was going to be Sheff's girl-friend, I couldn't also be Faith Thompson. I'd have to be someone else, this character I was making up to impress him. And that made me mad. I mean, I've worked hard at becoming a person I like. I'm not going to turn my whole personality in and exchange it for another, just for some guy. I mean, give me a break."

"But did you ever think that he might like the real you just fine if he got a chance to know her?" Dana asked.

Faith thought about this for a moment, stretching her legs out and propping them up on the end of her bed, then said, "If he does, fine. I'll be around here. So will he. Maybe we can be friends. But for now, I already have a guy in my life. And I'm not going to throw him over just because the Philadelphia Smoothie has arrived on campus. With Johnny, I can be myself. I'm telling you, these days when we've been fighting and I haven't gotten to talk to him have driven me crazy. Usually we talk all the time. We try out new thoughts on each other, test our feelings by expressing them to each other. I don't want to give that up."

Dana nodded.

"I think you made the right decision," she said. "And it's the one Madame Irene ad-vised."

"That's right," Faith said, a slow smile

spreading across her face. "I'm being to mine own self true."

Dana laughed and said, "Something like that."

"I think that also means I ought to get rid of these purple nails. And the leather pants. And this hairdo."

"Keep the hairdo," Dana said. "I like it."

"Hey," Faith said, "what was it *you* wanted to talk to *me* about?"

"Terry's got a girl back home," Dana said, figuring there was no use beating around the bush.

"True love?" Faith asked.

"From the sandbox to the tomb, apparently."

"I'm sorry," Faith said, giving Dana a pat on the head.

"Thanks."

"I'm also not sorry," Faith added.

"What!?" Dana was mad.

"Simmer down. Listen to me first. I've been watching you for nearly two years now and it's been one mad crush after another. As soon as you met Terry and told me you thought he was cute and nice, I knew you'd fall for him. Dana, I know I'm not a psychologist or anything, but I think maybe this whole thing with your dad leaving and all has left you feeling insecure. And I think you approach every new guy as some kind of test.

Will he like you? Can you get him to fall for you? Terry O'Shaughnessy just wanted to be your friend, but you couldn't see that because of this program you're on."

"You think this is really true?" Dana asked.

"I think something's out of whack when you've had half a dozen boyfriends and not one boy *friend*."

"I don't even have a boyfriend anymore," Dana moaned. "I broke up with Randy thinking Terry was a sure thing. Now here I am, all alone."

"Maybe it's a good place for you to be for a while," Faith said. "Give yourself time to clear out your brain. You've been moving pretty fast. You don't want to be played out by the time you're seventeen, ready to go into a convent or become a hermit."

Dana cracked up.

"I can just see me as a hermit. First morning I'd crawl out of my hut and say, 'Hey. Is there a Bloomingdale's around here?' " Then she got serious again. "I don't know. Maybe you're right about me. I can't really say I feel like Terry did me a big favor by turning up with this girl friend, though. It still hurts too much. I really like him, you know. Maybe he will turn out to be a boy *friend*. But if that's the case, I know I'm also going to be looking for a new *boyfriend*."

Faith laughed and said, "That should take

about two days. Say, you're not feeling bad about breaking off with Randy, are you?"

"Sad, not bad," Dana said. "I know I'm going to miss certain things about him, stuff we did together, his family. But it wasn't happening for me, and it was wrong to pretend that it was. He should be free to find someone who really appreciates him. I'm just trying to behave responsibly. Maturely, I guess."

"I know," Faith said. "Isn't it *hard*, though?!"

"Incredibly!" Dana said and the two of them started laughing.

"What are you two cackling about?" Shelley said, coming through the door, loaded down with books and a can of soda and a bag of cheese doodles.

They told her, then Dana suddenly remembered.

"Oh, gosh!" she exclaimed. "I almost forgot the juiciest detail. I know who the mad pranksters are. Terry told me. It was him and Sheff and Keith. Someone toilet-papered and shaving-creamed their room and made it look like we did it. So they were trying to get back at us."

"But who t.p.ed their room?" Shelley wondered.

"My guess," Dana said, "is three guys from the friendly town of Greenleaf."

"Those rats!" Faith said, jumping up.

"We'll get 'em. We'll get 'em good. Those country boys forgot they were messing with a girl from D.C. Growing up in the inner city, you learn the heavy duty pranks."

"Oh, we'll get them all right," Dana agreed. "But we can deal with the guys from Greenleaf later. First we have to help the boys of Canby Hall."

CHAPTER TWENTY

The next morning, it was pouring rain. Down in their basement room, Terry, Sheff, and Keith — on Dana's advice — decided to turn themselves in to Ms. Allardyce.

Before classes began, they ran across campus, getting soaked in the process, so that by the time they got to the shelter of the front porch of the headmistress' house, they looked like drowned rats. Terry pulled the chain that rang the old-fashioned doorbell.

Apparently it was her housekeeper's day off, as Ms. Allardyce answered the door herself. She seemed surprised to find the boys there.

"Yes?" she said, tentatively, but smiling. Clearly she wasn't expecting a confession.

The three of them had decided that Sheff would be their spokesman. He stepped forward and got right to the point.

"We're the ones responsible," he hesitated,

searching for an expression with the right spin on it, "for the unfortunate incident in the cafeteria yesterday. We were playing a prank on some girls we thought had vandalized our room. We were wrong that it was them, and we were wrong to play the prank. We're sorry."

Ms. Allardyce just nodded for a moment, then stepped back and was about to close the door in their faces when Keith stopped her.

"Wait," he called. "Aren't you going to say anything? Don't we get to find out what's going to happen to us?"

Ms. Allardyce smiled ever so sweetly and said, "Tomorrow. I have to think about this. You see, if it were just three of the girls, I could deal with them as individuals. But I'm afraid this incident has larger ramifications. If this is the sort of thing we can expect from boys, do we really want boys at Canby Hall at all — now or ever?"

When she shut the door, they watched it click in their faces. It was still raining heavily. They were still soaking wet. They'd just been told they might be thrown out of school and change back its co-ed status for once and for all.

"Well," Keith said, "look on the bright side."

"What possible bright side can there be?" Sheff asked.

"It's going to be a long time before they serve beef stroganoff around here again."

The other two cracked up. Keith's remark broke through their gloom.

"I say let's make the run back, get dry, find the girls, and come up with something we can do about this mess," Terry suggested.

"All *right*," Sheff said.

"All right," Keith said, imitating Sheff, but not coming close. He had a way with slang that made it sound like he was reading it out of *A Guide to Being Cool*.

At dusk that night, the seven of them — the roommates, Casey, and the boys — were sitting out in the clearing in the maple grove. They had all met in the cafeteria and come outside to try to think of some way to stop Ms. Allardyce from expelling the guys.

"I think what we need to do," Dana said, "is take her by surprise. Distract her from her thinking on the matter. Turn her around in her tracks."

"But what could do that?" Sheff asked.

"Something to show her we're reformed," Terry offered. "You know, starting fresh."

"That's it!" Faith cried. "A fresh start. P.A. just goes goony over spring and all its fresh starts. It's her main brain theme of the season."

"But how does that help us?" Shelley asked.

"Well . . ." Faith said, and began explaining her plan to the rest of them.

The next morning, Patrice Allardyce awoke to the sounds of a hundred birds at the birdbath outside her bedroom window.

"Ah," she said to herself, "spring." And then she sat up and swung her feet over the side and into the slippers waiting on the floor next to her bed. As she crossed the floor of her room in her buttercup yellow nightgown, she hummed the tune to "Oh, What a Beautiful Morning." When she got to the window of her room, which overlooked the large front lawn of the house, she stretched and yawned with her eyes closed. It wasn't until she opened them that she saw the surprise. She blinked a few times to make sure what she was seeing was real and not imaginary. But it was real, all right.

There on the lawn was the largest bouquet she had ever seen. It was at least ten feet in diameter, and the flowers were assembled in a color wheel that went from blue to violet to red to yellow to white.

Making up the stems of the bouquet were cut lengths of an old garden hose. Tying these together was a "ribbon" made of a long, wide sheet of hot pink crepe paper, knotted into a bow.

Standing next to the bouquet was a

propped-up piece of white cardboard, five feet square. On it was written, in huge black script, P. ALLARDYCE. PLEASE FORGIVE YOUR BAD BOYS.

Ms. Allardyce stood looking at this and for a long moment seemed simply astonished. Her mouth and eyes were wide open, her hand was at her throat.

And then she broke into a smile, then a laugh so hearty that Dana and Faith and Shelley and Casey and Sheff and Terry and Keith could all hear it from their various hiding places in the bushes and trees around the yard.

And to see it was to know that no one was going to be expelled from Canby Hall today.

Late that night, they all got together in the basement laundry room to celebrate Ms. Allardyce's decision to let the guys off with the penalty of doing yard work around the campus for the rest of the Saturdays in the term.

They were congratulating themselves on a brilliant stunt. They still couldn't quite believe they'd pulled it off. This afternoon, Faith had taken a picture of them all in front of the bouquet. She'd put her camera on a tripod, set the timer and jumped in front of it so she could be in the picture, too. She knew it would be one she'd want to have forever.

She looked around now at this laundry

room full of her best friends. Dana and Shelley were doing a soft shoe dance across the row of washers. Keith and Casey were sitting atop a dryer, holding hands. Terry was letting Sheff show him how to play a three-note song on the trumpet.

When they were done fooling around, it was Terry who said, "I guess the only unfinished business is what to do to those rotten Greenleaf twerps," he said.

"Don't you talk that way about my boyfriend," Faith said, in a mock huff. She did hope, though, that this would get the point across to Sheff that she had decided to go back to Johnny. He looked across the room at her and said, "Oh, so you're soft on them, eh?" he teased. "Don't want to do anything to hurt their little feelings?"

Faith laughed, "Are you kidding? Just because I don't want anyone to call them twerps doesn't mean I'm going to go the least bit light on them. Did you all know, for instance, that there's a watercolor paint that comes off, but when it's on a person's car could fool him into thinking it's the real thing? I mean, for openers, how do you think they'll enjoy waking up next Saturday to find their precious automobiles are all chartreuse with purple tops?"

The others rubbed their hands in villainish glee, and they all began planning Operation Double Cross.

* * *

Later that evening Dana, Faith, and Shelley were sitting on top of their mattresses. It was almost lights out and there was just enough time to finish one last snack.

"Boys on campus," Dana sighed. "They're a lot of trouble. . . ."

"But not more trouble than they're worth," Shelley finished for her, with a grin.

"I don't know about that," Faith said. "I never realized how lucky I was when all I had to worry about was Johnny Bates."

"I always knew how lucky I've been in roommates but now I know I can depend on you two to see me through anything," Dana said.

"Well, almost anything," Shelley added, as she switched off the light.

"Yeah. Not another boyfriend," Faith said, laughing. "At least not for a few weeks."

"Months!" Shelley said and pulled the covers over her head.